JEAN ROSS JUSTICE

On the Life and Work
of an American Master

ISBN: 978-1-7344356-2-7

Published by The Unsung Masters Series in collaboration with *Gulf Coast,*
Copper Nickel, Pleiades, and *The Georgia Review.*

Department of English
University of Houston
Houston, TX 77204

Produced at the University of Houston Department of English

Distributed by Small Press Distribution (SPD) and to subscribers of *Pleiades:*
Literature in Context, Gulf Coast: A Journal of Literature and Fine Arts, and *The Georgia Review.*

Series, cover, and interior design and layout by Martin Rock.
Cover photograph courtesy of the family of Jean Ross Justice.

2 4 6 8 9 7 5 3 1
First Printing, 2022

The Unsung Masters Series brings the work of great, out-of-print, little-known
writers to new readers. Each volume in the Series includes a large selection of
the author's original writing, as well as essays on the writer, interviews with
people who knew the writer, photographs, and ephemera. The curators of the
Unsung Masters Series are always interested in suggestions for future volumes.

Invaluable financial support for this project
has been provided by the Nancy Luton Fund;
and the University of Houston English Department.

UNIVERSITY of **HOUSTON**

JEAN ROSS JUSTICE

On the Life and Work
of an American Master

Edited by RYAN BOLLENBACH
and KEVIN PRUFER

Shreela Ray: On the Life and Work of an American Master
Edited by Kazim Ali & Rohan Chhetri

Wendy Battin: On the Life and Work of an American Master
Edited by Charles Hartman, Martha Collins, Pamela Alexander,
& Matthew Krajniak

Laura Hershey: On the Life & Work of an American Master
Edited by Meg Day & Niki Herd

Adelaide Crapsey: On the Life and Work of an American Master
Edited by Jenny Molberg & Christian Bancroft

Belle Turnbull: On the Life & Work of an American Master
Edited by David Rothman & Jeffrey Villines

Beatrice Hastings: On the Life & Work of Modern Master
Edited by Benjamin Johnson & Erika Jo Brown

Catherine Breese Davis: On the Life & Work of an American Master
Edited by Martha Collins, Kevin Prufer, & Martin Rock

Francis Jammes: On the Life & Work of a Modern Master
Edited by Kathryn Nuernberger and Bruce Whiteman

Russell Atkins: On the Life & Work of an American Master
Edited by Kevin Prufer & Michael Dumanis

Nancy Hale: On the Life & Work of a Lost American Master
Edited by Dan Chaon, Norah Hardin Lind & Phong Nguyen

Tamura Ryuichi: On the Life & Work of a 20th Century Master
Edited by Takako Lento & Wayne Miller

Dunstan Thompson: On the Life & Work of a Lost American Master
Edited by D. A. Powell & Kevin Prufer

Laura Jensen: A Symposium
Edited by Wayne Miller & Kevin Prufer

THE UNSUNG MASTERS SERIES

gULF COASt
A JOURNAL OF LITERATURE AND FINE ARTS

IN COLLABORATION WITH

THE GEORGIA REVIEW

Cu 29 Ni 28

PLEIADES
PRESS

CONTENTS

INTRODUCTION

SHORT STORIES

ESSAYS

INTRODUCTION

BY WAY OF INTRODUCTION:
AN INTERVIEW WITH NAT JUSTICE

Nat Justice is the son of Jean Ross Justice and the poet Donald Justice. This interview was conducted via email and recorded conversation in December of 2021.

Unsung Masters Series: Before we begin to talk about your mother, can you tell us something about yourself?

Nat Justice: Sure thing. I'll just give you the thumbnail sketch. I live in Black Mountain, North Carolina, which is the same place where my mother first wanted to go to school, at Black Mountain College. I've been retired for quite a while now and have been happily married for nearly twenty-five years. I'm an amateur musician—guitar, drums, piano in descending order of proficiency. And I wrote a couple novels. Well, I toyed around with them a lot, then decided they weren't all that great. I didn't try to publish them.

But, you know, observing my own parents write gave me a real appreciation for the craft and effort that go into creating a work of literature. And it may have been that my parents' roles as writers of more mainstream work influenced me to go in a different direction—my style was sort of Sam Spade meets Thomas Pynchon.

But mostly I've been enjoying life here and am very happy that my parents are remembered as they are.

UMS: Tell us about your mother's childhood.

NJ: My mother was born in 1924 and grew up in central North Carolina, on the family farm ("the old home place," as she called it) just outside the small town of Norwood. She was the youngest of four children; by the time I was old enough to remember, her parents were in failing health, so I didn't see her interact with them that much.

I know she loved her parents, but I think they may have been a little more old-fashioned and distant with their children, in a 19th-century sort of way. Both her parents were quite religious, but none of their children were, at least not in any devout way. I know she got along very well with her siblings, especially her sister Eleanor (later Eleanor Ross Taylor), and I think she had a happy childhood, all in all. The family was poor during the Depression, when she was growing up. She had memories of playing in an automobile in the barn; her father had bought it in the middle 1920s, but by about 1930 or so (when she was five or six), there was no longer enough money to keep it running and so it sat in the barn for a few years while they used a horse-drawn wagon, until times got better by the late 1930s.

Eleanor and Jean, on the family farm, about 1937

All her siblings were writers—I have to confess that I don't really know *why* all of them had that bug, but her oldest brother, James, who was about a dozen years older, had already had a novel published by 1940 (when she was about 16), so that would certainly have been a demonstration that some sort of writing career was possible (despite some good reviews, that novel, *They Don't Dance Much*, was the only one he ever published, so maybe not *that* possible).

She and Eleanor were the youngest, and so were still at home after the two older brothers had left home. Mom described how the two of them would be very excited by the delivery of the various magazines (*Saturday Evening Post, Liberty, Colliers*) that featured fiction. This would have been the later 1930s, by which time the family was doing somewhat better financially. Even so, a magazine subscription was a noticeable expense.

I know that she was interested in attending Black Mountain College because it was so avant-garde and forward thinking, but instead went to the University of North Carolina (where she met my father a couple of years later, in grad school). I'm not clear on (and sadly never asked her about) exactly how the family was able to afford college. (I don't think either brother finished a degree, although again, I may be mistaken on that.)

(Years later, my dad would laugh about her wanting to go to Black Mountain. He'd say she was so lucky she didn't get in because . . . well, he didn't mean that those guys were a bunch of stumble bums *exactly*, but she knew what he meant.)

I know she worked in defense plants (inspecting shells, among other things) during the war, and it may be that that helped save up some money.

I think she had only faint memories of her grandparents, in part because she was the baby of the family and they would have been older by the time she was old enough to remember them.

UMS: It must have been strange for your mother to have three other siblings who were also writers, especially Eleanor Ross Taylor, who is such an important poet. Can you describe their relationship?

NJ: Oh, yes, they were very close. But at the same time they were competitive with each other and other writers. Their lives had similar trajectories. They both married much more famous male writers, for instance. They both paid close attention to others writers—whose stock was up, whose stock was down, that kind of thing.

When the four of them—my father and mother and Eleanor and Peter [Taylor]—got together, there was a lot of talk about who was publishing what and where. They'd say things like, well, "what did you think of the latest John Cheever story in *The New Yorker?*" "Oh, not that much." "Or the new William Styron novel?" "Just a mess. He needs an editor." Those kinds of conversations happened all the time with the four of them.

And given that, I can only imagine that they were pretty aware of each other's stock—I mean, in a competitive way, but not a *very* competitive way. Not an unfriendly way.

UMS: When did you first become aware of your parents as writers?

NJ: I think I first became aware of them as writers when I was in my early teens. It didn't seem particularly unusual to me, of course; there were always a lot of books everywhere we lived, and a lot of their conversation (not all of which I paid attention to, but which I was always sort of absorbing) was about writers and books, about who was underrated and who was overrated, things like that. So being a writer as a pursuit seemed like quite a reasonable and familiar thing.

It may be that the first of her stories that I ever read was "So Long, Tenderfoot," which I found a memorably odd title; I think this would have been about 1980 or so, when I was still a teenager. I liked the stories, although I'm not quite sure I was old enough at the time to understand them; in one of the stories, one secondary character is a mopey teenager playing a boardgame (Panzerblitz) which I'd played a lot of a few years earlier. I found it a slightly unsettling feeling, as though I'd caught a glimpse of myself in a mirror I hadn't known was there.

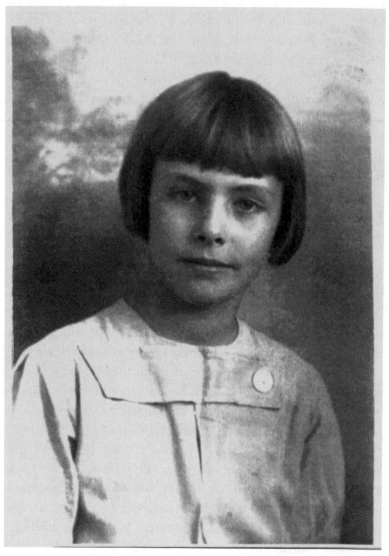

Jean Ross at 8 or 9 years of age, about 1932

UMS: Do you see other echoes of your own family in your mother's fiction?

NJ: Only in the most superficial fashion. She was always very interested in what television I was watching, what bands I was listening to. Did I listen to them on cassette? Or on vinyl? She used her observations of the family to get details right, a turn of phrase, set-design, so to speak. But I don't think she modeled her stories on the family very much. My feeling is that she wasn't looking to us to get emotional or familial details right for her fiction. My family life was stable and undramatic. But, then again, I was a kid. A lot may have gone right over my head.

UMS: Was your household often visited by other writers when you were growing up?

NJ: I can rattle off some names, without being able to say much about most of them. There weren't constant parties, but my parents did like to entertain a bit. I have a memory of locking Kurt Vonnegut out of the house at a party in the mid-1960s. He'd stepped out on the back porch of the house we lived in (in Syracuse, New York, I think) to smoke a cigarette (or maybe a joint? in the mid-1960s, stepping outside to smoke a cigarette would have been unusual, I'd think?), and five-year-old me thought locking the door behind him would be a good idea. He eventually got back in and seemed fairly good-natured about it.

I heard *stories* about John Berryman, who on one occasion made an intoxicated pass at my mom (she apparently deflected him without difficulty), about Philip Roth (who seemed prickly and unpleasant, especially with his then-wife, Claire Bloom; I remember that when I heard my parents discussing them, I was more impressed by the Movie Star name-drop than by the Famous Writer name-drop). Also, Philip Roth: not as good a poker player as he thought he was; Nelson Algren: first-rate poker player. Probably not the most significant metric for their literary reputations, but there you go.

And of course we saw a lot of Eleanor and her husband, Peter Taylor, himself a writer of note. I liked Eleanor and Peter a lot, but it was always funny to me as a kid how much more Southern the two of them sounded than did my parents (my mother had a definite but very soft Southern accent, and my dad, despite being from Florida, hardly had one at all).

UMS: Did she talk about her work as a writer with you?

NJ: She didn't talk that much about her process as a writer. I do remember that she'd sometimes make a fairly close study of a particular story or section from a novel that had impressed her (unfortunately, I can't come up with any examples at the moment); she'd see how much of the plot was advanced by dialog, how much by narration, that sort of thing. She was very disciplined about setting aside time every day to write, and I think also to read. She would rarely abandon a novel she'd started reading, even if she was finding it slow going, or not really liking it. I used to tease her about that (it seems like German writers were the worst, or at least I remember her slogging dutifully through *Dr. Faustus* and *The Tin Drum* without any particular love for the books).

UMS: She didn't publish her first books until she was in her 80s, and then quickly published two books of stories and self-published a novel. What was her relationship with the world of publishing like?

NJ: Well, she sent the novel around a little bit, then wound up self-publishing it. I helped her out a bit with the formatting and design.

But in general, she did try to publish, yes, but she found it frustrating. And for much of the years she was writing, she was also looking after my father, who was in poor health. It wasn't until he died that she had more time to focus on her own work. And then, frustrated, she decided that the kind of work she was writing wasn't all that fashionable or marketable, and because she was a woman in her late 70s and 80s, *she* wasn't that marketable, either.

She was very self-critical. But at the same time, she was very critical of what was being published. *The New Yorker* would arrive and she'd read the stories and say, well, I guess this is the fashion these days. It's not what I'm doing. And it's not very good. She had a little disdain for much of it.

UMS: How else did she like to spend her day?

NJ: Most of my memories of her when I was young were just of her being "mom" and taking care of me; I do remember that she was always a voracious reader, although unlike my present-day habit, she'd focus like a laser on one novel and power through it. She and my father shared a number of artistic interests—they both liked paintings (and visiting art museums), were both movie buffs, and both enjoyed travel. I don't think they saw eye to eye on music; my dad liked spikier 20th-century Modernist stuff (as well as Bach and Chopin), but after his death I remember my mom playing some old gospel hymns ("Shall We Gather at the River") on the piano.

Once I was high-school age (late 1970s), the three of us used to go to the University of Iowa film series a lot, seeing a mix of classic Hollywood, silent films, European and Japanese art film, and recent artsier movies. This was pre-VCR, much less streaming, so we wound up talking a lot about the movies, and my parents would mention films they'd seen years ago that had made an impression on them. Both my parents had a lot of recollections of going to the movies when they were younger; I think they were of the prime movie-going generation and had vivid memories of what they'd seen in college and grad school (Bette Davis in *Now, Voyager*, and then a few years later, Bogart and Bacall in *Dark Passage*).

UMS: Do you remember what writers she regarded most highly?

NJ: A very partial list, off the top of my head, and doubtless forgetting a lot (and I may have referenced some of these earlier): Joyce (definitely up through *Dubliners* and *Portrait of the Artist*; possibly *Ulysses*, but none of that *Finnegan's Wake* nonsense); Nabokov (his stories, especially, rather than the novels, which she felt leaned into the bizarre a little too hard); Barbara Pym; Faulkner (she was always fascinated by his work, but I think eventually thought of him as a kind of hothouse flower, and probably a bad influence on other writers' styles); George Eliot (*Middlemarch* was among her favorite novels); D. H. Lawrence, both the novels and the

The Ross siblings: James, Eleanor, Jean, and Fred, in about 1975

stories. Chekhov and Tolstoy, but not Dostoyevsky, at least not so much (I think *The Possessed* was another of the long novels that turned into a bit of a slog for her).

She read more fiction than history, but I do remember her taking an interest in Russia, especially old, pre-First World War Russia (I think in part because Nabokov's *Speak, Memory* was one of her favorite memoirs). We had some coffee-table photography books of c.1900 Russia that I recall fondly.

UMS: What do you recall about your mother's work habits as a writer?

NJ: As far as I noticed, she was always very diligent and very disciplined. As far back as I can recall (including, I think, our rented houses in Syracuse and in Laguna Beach) she had a small space set aside as her work area, with a typewriter and a small desk. Even later on, in the sprawling house in Gainesville and the big house in Iowa City, she wound up picking a rather small room to use as her office, I think by preference. She liked having a cozy space, with room for her typewriter (manual), a couple of notebooks and maybe a manila folder or two for newspaper clippings, a small selection of books (I remember a lot of Chekhov, *Dubliners*, and William Trevor, but I'm sure I'm forgetting many more), and a photograph of her parents.

I recall that she liked having her study a little out of the way. We'd usually have cartons of books in the basements and garages of our houses, but she'd have one modest-sized bookshelf in the study. (One of the books that was usually there was Nabokov's *Lectures on Russian Literature*.)

UMS: Did she talk to you about her writing?

NJ: I know that she took writing very seriously and thought about her style, her manner, a great deal. She enjoyed working at the craft of writing. Insofar as we talked about writing, a lot of the time it was to discuss other writers' strengths and weaknesses. I think one aspect of writing that she was always thinking about was plot; she'd have newspaper clippings about various small-town crimes that she thought might work as ideas for fiction (a couple of murders, also a banker cleaning out the savings & loan before skipping town, and probably some others I've forgotten). At one point, she and my father drove over to the next county a couple of times to attend a couple of days of a murder trial she was interested in making some fictional use of (I think she wanted to see the faces of a couple of the "characters" when they testified).

UMS: Did she speak much about what it meant to her to be a female writer or how she perceived the status of female writers changing?

NJ: First, a caveat that my memories of her as a working writer are fragmentary and incomplete, so I'm sure I'm leaving out some things that were important to her, but I don't think I'm misrepresenting anything. I think my mother was, artistically speaking, rather solitary by nature. At least on occasion, she'd show things to my dad to get his thoughts (and he would do the same with her, when he had a poem he'd been tinkering with and wasn't sure about—the "is this worth going on with?" sort of thing, I think).

I'm not certain, but wouldn't be in the least surprised if she did something similar with her sister Eleanor. My mother also, like my father, had a fairly slow and drawn-out artistic process; she had stories or bits of novels that she'd had lying around for a year or two, and would then return to with a fresh idea. I *think* that for the most part she would just keep polishing a piece of fiction until she was happy with it, rather than workshop it or share it with many other people.

She was certainly aware of herself as a female writer, and I think also aware of being married to a well-known male writer. I always felt like there had been a conscious decision between the two of them that they'd work different beats, so to speak. My dad had a short story published in the *O. Henry Awards* anthology in about 1950, but after that I don't know that he ever wrote prose fiction again.

I don't know that my mom ever wrote much (any?) poetry (sort of the reverse of the situation with her sister, where Eleanor wrote the all poetry, and Peter Taylor wrote the novels and stories). I don't know to what degree she thought of herself as a female writer; I think to some extent, certainly, but in the same way I think she thought of herself as to some extent a Southern writer.

UMS: Did your mother consider herself to be a "Southern" writer in the ways Southern writers of her generation are often discussed today?

NJ: Only to an extent. I've been thinking about that a lot. It was an aspect of her identity for sure, but she didn't want to be pigeonholed that way—as a Southern writer, as a female writer. She thought of herself as a writer.

She was a huge fan of Eudora Welty, as was my father. Flannery O'Connor, on the other hand, she thought was a little baroque, a little over-the-top. She and my father shared their likes and dislikes so much—there was so much overlap. It was hard sometimes to tell who was in the lead when it came to their mutual tastes.

UMS: What role did friendship or non-familial relationships play in her life?

NJ: I honestly don't know the answer to that. . . . I think she was a fairly reserved person (I'm that way, and I think I get it more from her than from my dad), but she certainly had some good friends when I was growing up. I think most of the friendships I was aware of were more about everyday things (comparing notes with a female friend on how the kids are doing in junior high) than anything particularly artistic or literary.

You know, I have great memories of my mother. She was steeped in history, in geography. She loved to think about

Jean and Don, and Hugo the dog, summer 1961

the past, how people arrived at their present situation. She had a historian's mind in a lot of ways, and a deep interest in the past. I remember driving around with her in Norwood, North Carolina, where the family had been for generations. She'd point to a farmhouse and say, this was uncle so-and-so's place where there was a family reunion in 1915. Or we'd visit cemeteries and she'd tell me who was buried here and there, maybe some old guy from two farms down the road. The past was always present for her. People's histories were always interesting to her.

UMS: Why do you think she never found a wide audience during her lifetime?

NJ: Well, her work didn't have sizzle. It wasn't fashionable. If you think success has to do with novelty or innovation, then, well, she wasn't well suited to that. She was very much *in* the tradition and not interested in innovation. She wasn't a self-promoter.

Look, both of my parents were ambitious, but my father much more so when it came to public success. He worried about career, legacy, readership; she had some perspective on that and it didn't seem to eat at her much. The work satisfied her. And being appreciated by a few good people seemed to satisfy her, too.

And I know it's pretty easy to say she gave up her career to help his, but I think that's not really true. It's much more complicated. He was ambitious for his own work and very capable. He didn't need a lot of encouragement. And he was also very supportive of her work. And they kept their work separate. His purview was poetry; hers was fiction.

UMS: The poet Russell Atkins, the subject of a previous volume in this series, once rather sardonically said that being an "unsung master" is both damnation and high praise. What would your mother have thought about being the subject of this book?

NJ: Oh, she'd have been delighted. Absolutely delighted. I was going to say she'd have been delighted *also* to sell a million copies of her novel—but, you know, I'm not sure about that, on second thought. She was a wonderful woman and I say this with all the love in the world—but she could also be a bit of a snob. And there's something very refined about being an "unsung master," like she might be a little too difficult for the rabble to appreciate, but the refined could understand her. They'd get it.

SHORT STORIES

DOUBLE FIRST COUSINS

Twice today my life was spared. The first close call was at the river bridge, when I was making a left turn. I'd misjudged the speed of the oncoming car and was barely out of the way in time; he blasted me with the horn. The sound spread out on the air, flat and metallic. I had a brief palpitation, a feeling like a small bicyclist deep in my chest, pedaling too fast, whirling away. If there'd been a crash, I'd have said to the police: my fault, all my fault!

I'm an old woman driving a long burgundy car, one of those powerful gas-guzzlers, the last car my husband, Norris, picked out. That deep, rich hum he liked is worn out; the engine has come to have an unhealthy, excitable sound.

But this morning I was spared again. They're gone, the others, Gwen and Kip and Norris; they're all dead. No, it was not some mass tragedy: they got old, they died. I got old;

I'm still here. Kip died quite suddenly, at his wife Gwen's care center; he'd gone there to have lunch with her. I didn't see him often in his old age, but remember his relatives with their reddish cheeks, clumping along on stiff legs, their voices loud from deafness, and so I can picture him pushing her wheelchair into the dining room, making his way slowly, or perhaps an aide is pushing her. The aide leaves; they're, in a sense, alone together in the big room of small tables with white tablecloths. They talk a little, as quietly as deafness allows. They eat; everyone eats; there's a clatter of dishes. He rises at the end, after the cottage pudding, and falls— blam. An aide runs over, another is running to the hall, calling. He's gone. Gwen sits in the wheelchair, watching. That's how it ended; and I hold onto that picture of them, an old couple lunching together and at least imitating, there in their last years, a peaceful life together.

I went there to help, after her diagnosis. People said, "How wonderful of you to go help out," and I said, "Wouldn't you do the same for somebody that close to you?" We were double first cousins: in our parents' generation, two sisters had married brothers. We'd grown up down the road from each other, always together.

First, let me explain how it was there in the country. Kip's family lived down on the river. In my childhood, "down on the river" sounded tony and romantic. Perhaps my father, saying the words, sounded envious. That was where the good land was, and it was true that the families who lived down there were old families and reasonably prosperous, even during the Depression. We saw their cars pass at a time when ours sat in the garage for lack of money to buy a tag. And Gwen and I lived in books and imagination: we read Agatha

Christie and dreamed of the Calais coach and the Orient Express; of New York, where the women in magazine stories lived, owed their furriers, remembered boarding school at St. Cloud, and received telegrams and flowers. We weren't like my high school friend, Mary Alice, who'd married a hard-working, loud-mouthed dairy farmer, but even with the work and early rising finished a book or two a week; she read them fast but didn't dream over them. She'd grasped something important: that her life had nothing to do with anything in books, a distinction Gwen and I had been careless of. Kip's home down on the river, genuinely old, with genuine old two-story-high columns, seemed to us a romantic place where something in a book might happen. And he was good-looking and sure of himself. She married him and lived down on the river, and found it was as dull as anywhere else. Then she got sick, and I lived there a while too.

"Nothing ever happens down here," Gwen used to say to me. "You ought not to be wasting your life here, Marguerite. Go back to college. Get your application in for the fall before it's too late."

"I love it here," I said.

I went to help. I worked; she worried. She worked some too; her weakness came and went. She sat at the kitchen table peeling vegetables or finding the right recipe in the cookbook. But sometimes she sighed, sitting there at the table, and sometimes her hands trembled; she had dizzy spells. She lay down at odd times, and her naps might last all afternoon.

Her mother, Aunt Georgia, said, "I think it's partly worrying about it, don't you?" She came over as often as she could; she had a good deal of stomach trouble and had aged early. "They've scared her. If she could take the burden to the

33

Lord—I'm praying." I didn't pray; instead, I told Gwen not to worry, it would be all right. I worked, and waited for Kip to get home in the afternoons.

Gwen was impatient with the illness; she was simply trying to pass the time till she was well again. She saw it that way, like a jail term that would end. I see us sitting at a card table in the early November twilight, working on a jigsaw puzzle. Once in a while she would stop and stare off into the distance, as if thinking, *So this is what it's like, being grown up and married.* We worked on the puzzle and waited for Kip.

When Kip came into a room, he took charge, and you knew interesting things would start happening and your life would be different for at least a little while. He approached the world with a companionable intensity. "Ladies!" he'd cry, coming into the house from work, "how are the Strickland girls this pip-Emma?" (We liked these little Briticisms.) "How's my beautiful wife?" He might take up the binoculars and look for birds along the river, and point out the evening colors of the sky. Sometimes he'd have stopped by the library to get a travel book full of pictures, or an art book or a book of photographs. He would put some music on the turntable, and gently move his arm, conducting it. We could do these things ourselves, of course; we picked up the binoculars too, and sometimes listened to music, but it was better when Kip was in charge. He told Gwen she was beautiful, but she wasn't exactly beautiful. She was what was called in those days "cute," with a thinnish, pointed face and darting dark eyes behind glasses. She and Kip were several years apart in age; they'd been sweethearts at college, a college over in the mountains, a long way from home; being from the same place had drawn them together.

Those evenings Gwen often didn't find much to say—what was there to talk about? The waffles we had for lunch, and her nap, and the puzzle we were working on? Kip was the one who talked. "What do you think Tenzing Norgay is doing at this moment? What time would it be in Nepal?" or, "What is Marilyn Monroe eating tonight?"

"Not much," I said. "I bet she's hardly eating anything at all. They have to watch their figures."

Kip and I played ping-pong out on the side porch. "Sure, go ahead," Gwen said. "You need the exercise, Kip—you're going to get fat, sitting so much at work." Now I am able to imagine her off in the living room, hearing us on the porch: the hollow plink as the balls bounced on the table, my giggles and screams as I missed shots, not being a good player; Kip's little high-pitched "Ee-yow!" Now I can imagine it.

I asked Kip which pictures he liked in the art books he'd brought home; I wanted to know what he thought about everything. I got him to tell me about his time in the Air Corps during the war, about flying over the Alps from Italy to Munich to take out an airfield and running into German planes, wheeling the gun around to fire at a German 109 flying beside him as if in formation, then seeing it drop away. There was the time when a navigator got them off course, and they barely made it back on the fuel they had. Hearing these things thrilled me to weakness.

"And I'd think, good God, I've got to do this thirty more times before I get to go home!" he said.

Gwen listened too and made little murmurs, but sometimes she had a magazine on her lap, turning the pages. I suppose she'd heard it all before.

He made up word games, such as thinking up expressions with the word *dark*. "Dark as night. Dark as Egypt, my mother used to say. Referring to the plagues in the Bible. Dark as—what?"

"Dark as a storm cloud," Gwen said. "Dark as my future."

One night he asked us what we remembered from first grade, and who our favorite teachers had been.

"How about the most unforgettable character we ever met!" Gwen said scornfully. "Oh, God, all these games, oh, God. Listen, I'm so tired of all this." She began to cry. Kip got up and put his arms around her. I got up too, and stood by awkwardly. "I'm sorry, please excuse me, I'm sick. Maybe we ought to move, maybe it's down here that's part of it. Excuse me, I'm sorry."

"Don't worry, you're excused," Kip said. "Want some tea? Want to play Scrabble?"

"No, I'm okay. You're sweet." She laughed hoarsely. "That was silly. It was silly about moving too. I'm sorry, I don't want to be like that."

She went to bed early. I sat on in the living room, halfway reading, and when Kip came back after seeing her to bed, I said, "She's not herself. I know it's hard on you—I'm sorry." He pursed his lips with a little shrug, then remembered to smile.

Kip's mother, Mrs. Treadway, came regularly. She'd yielded up the old house with the columns to Kip and Gwen, and gone to live in town after her husband died. She livened a place up—like Kip, but not like him. She came in already talking in her loud voice, almost taking charge; I imagined her as good at directing pageants or party games. Often she brought food, part of a ham or some stew or a pie. "So sweet of her," I said. Gwen said, "Sure. Partly, she's afraid we're not feeding him well enough. But that's okay."

Mrs. Treadway had a smooth, plump face, and sat with her legs stretched out before her, her ankles crossed; she gave off several sweet scents at once. She told us the local gossip, and stories from years past. Some businessman in Eady had run off with a woman he worked with, and that led her to a man she'd known in her working days. "Stepped out on his wife all the time! He'd go out at night and stay gone quite a while, and when he got home his wife would ask where he'd been. 'What d'you think, out with a blonde, of course,' and she'd have to laugh, so he got out of it like that—but it was where he'd been, all right."

"So this fellow had an affair for five long years, and kept it quiet! It's usually their secretaries, isn't it. Somebody they work with."

"Don't worry," Gwen said with a lazy air. "Miss Bertha"— Kip's office help at the courthouse—"is homely as a mud fence, and twenty-odd years older than he is." Mrs. Treadway squealed, "Oh, honey!" as if Gwen had said something extra-witty, or as if she herself had been found out doing something cute but risky.

To me she said, "Not many girls would sacrifice their college years like this. I see the styles in the Charlotte paper, the going-back-to-school things, so cute." She would look at me searchingly. "Don't put it off too long, honey. It gets too hard to go back." My going was her other topic, along with the faithlessness of men. I'd never have guessed that she thought about college that much; Kip was the only one in her family who'd gone. She knew our family was "smart," of course, but to her that was just another characteristic, like "tall" or "brown-haired."

I will admit that what I remember about Gwen's physical condition that winter is chiefly what Kip said about it. "Her dizziness is getting a little worse," he said the night of her little blowup. "I don't want her to fall. Think she'd use a cane if I got one?"

"I could try to talk her into it."

"Maybe if I got a really handsome one. . . . Well, she doesn't seem a whole lot worse, but it's hard to tell."

It was the next summer when we heard that a preacher was conducting healing services at a revival meeting in a little backwoods church.

I was surprised when Gwen said one night, "Let's go hear that preacher—the healer? I always wanted to know what they did, if they ranted and hollered, or what. It'll be an experience."

A hot August evening. We drove over unfamiliar country roads, fields of high corn often walling us in on both sides; we rattled over creeks on plank bridges. "The creek's low," Kip said. "Wonder if they're praying for rain." The houses were farther apart out here, and I felt the landscape had been unchanged for years; the farms seemed to lie there in a deep calm. A calm seemed to lie over us, too; we didn't talk much.

The church, when we found it, was as it must have been seventy years before: white, square and squat, on brick legs exposing the space under it; wooden steps up to two separate doors. The people were going in. I thought they might give us hard looks, strangers in simple, sporty summer clothes, not their Sunday dress-up style; I thought they'd see through us and know we were there from curiosity. But they didn't give us hard looks; they understood Gwen better than I did.

We'd gone back to childhood. Back to the time when we took for granted the exhortations from the pulpit during revival week, and the tears of sinners at the altar, as often as not just some nervous teenage girl whose parents had instructed her that it was time to join the church. Back to the days before we'd begun to note and treasure the preacher's mispronunciations and shaky grammar. Now we sat on the hard benches of an even more primitive church than ours, among the kind of people we'd known forever but were sure we were different from; poor, taciturn, freshly washed people who'd sung doggedly from these worn hymnals through flush times and bad, singing about rescuing the perishing and showers of blessings. The church had an odd dry smell, like ancient paper or the dusty burlap curtains on wires that were used to separate the classes for Sunday School.

Then the preaching. The preacher was not young—tall, a bit stooped, his hair at the temples flaring white against the dark gray, as if it had been dusted with cornstarch for the stage. His suit coat hung long, as if too large; he took it off and folded it fastidiously over the chair behind the pulpit, stripping for action. He had a powerful voice.

At the end of the sermon he invited those in search of healing to come forward. "O Lord, we call on the healing power of Jesus of Nazareth—"

All around the church people rose, as if dutifully. Some of them were helping other people to their feet. A young couple went up the aisle, a pink blanket trailing from the baby in the man's arms; a middle-aged man in a short-sleeved white shirt helped an old woman whose hip moved with an odd rotating motion.

"The baby's sickly," the woman beside me whispered, without looking at me. I nodded. And I saw with uneasy surprise that my cousin was getting to her feet.

From the back of the church a woman shouted, "Bless the Lord, bless his holy name!"

"What's the matter with her?" the woman whispered.

"Multiple sclerosis. They *say*." The woman nodded wisely at "they say." What did *they* know! And I was glad for this whispering woman, for I felt left alone as Gwen and Kip made their way up the aisle.

Up the aisle! At their wedding they'd walked up the aisle together. A simple wedding, at Christmastime. Gwen had planned it, and might have modeled it on a wedding she'd read about long ago in *The Charlotte Observer*: in adolescence she'd kept a scrapbook of her favorite weddings from the Sunday paper. Poinsettias and holly, red candles flickering, Gwen in a white velveteen dress her mother had made; her parents snuffling off and on. "Bet it makes you think about when you're gonna get married," one of my cousins said afterward, but it didn't. How could I ever match *this* wedding? I imagined them lounging in each other's arms, by firelight, dreamy and perfect, as in a magazine illustration.

That early evening in the country church the preacher was praying over the old woman with the bad hip. Kip and Gwen came next. Kip murmured something to the preacher, and they knelt at the altar rail. The preacher's voice went a little softer. "Oh, Lord, grant us tonight thy merciful healing power. . . ."

I closed my eyes and tried to shift my thoughts to something else. But tears had come; I was moved against my will. The woman beside me whispered, "I'll pray for her."

In the car on the way home Gwen was jolly. "What a voice he had! That's the secret, their voices. The power of suggestion, it's like hypnosis. It can work sometimes. Actually

I feel better already." She pretended she was joking, but I knew her; she wasn't joking. I should have understood then what she was going through.

Kip and I went blackberry picking one Saturday that summer. "We'll make you a pie," I said to Gwen. "You used to say it was your favorite." The blackberries grew wild along ditches and the railroad right-of-way. "I'm taking Kip along to keep off the snakes."

"Ah, Kip the snake killer," Kip said. "Let's hope we don't step on any."

"You don't need to do that. I don't need a pie," Gwen said. She looked positively distressed. "You'll get a lot of redbug bites, that's all. You don't need to!"

"They're just going to waste," I said. "We won't be gone long."

A beautiful hot day, the berries at their peak. I was happy to go tramping off with Kip. I don't remember what we talked about, maybe about picking huckleberries in the woods in the spring; maybe I told him about the time we'd found some frog legs in a brown paper bag by the side of the road when we were out looking for huckleberries. Whatever we talked about, it probably wasn't Gwen. I remember that she seemed somewhat sulky the rest of the day.

"You've let another fall go by, honey," Mrs. Treadway said to me in the kitchen, where she was stacking her gifts of food in the refrigerator. "When do you have to get your application in for the next year? Is it in the spring?"

"She needs me," I said. "We're *compatible*. She doesn't want some boring workhorse. It's pretty dull for her down here."

She raised her eyebrows. "Why's it so dull? She's got Kip. And people come." They did, occasionally, old married classmates, and in between keeping their kids out of mischief, they told her about having a TV set now, and about other people's doctors and illnesses. "Well, I think you better think about the future. It's more important than you may know. I've seen it happen. . . ."

She didn't say what she'd seen happen. I couldn't understand this obsession. Maybe she was a little batty. I could see her thinking about it half the time when she looked at me: You've got to go, you've got to go.

My boyfriend, Norris, wrote from college, and conscientiously reported his double dates ("to do a friend a favor"); according to him, he was indifferent to all the girls he dated. "She was a hard looker, I can tell you." He came home on weekends and took me out. "A real nice family," he'd say, speaking of Kip's folks as we drove away from the house. "One of the pioneer families, you know, they've had that mill forever. It's *historic*." We held hands in the movies and kissed goodnight. I felt that we were like some old married couple, comfortable, rather sure of one another, and that Kip and Gwen, back in the house, were the young lovers, still full of unresolved passion, still working things out. I'd wonder what they'd been saying or doing in my absence.

One morning in December, after Kip left for work, Gwen and I took off. She wanted to go somewhere, and there was a second car, the one she'd used in her job as a reading consultant for the county schools. We went out through the still chill morning, past the limp and withered vegetation of the yard, silvered with frost, and she headed for the driver's side. "It's okay. I feel pretty good today."

We went up our county road to the paved road and turned south through sparsely settled country, once the country of big "plantations," now too far from town for easy access to a job. A woman sweeping a front porch stopped and stared at us, and her dog ran out, eager for a car to chase. Down to the river bridge, a kingfisher high on a wire, and then we were in the next county. Farm fields and small poor houses; little towns with one or two fine old houses and then more fields; defunct one-room roadside stores, side roads with hand-lettered signs for fruits long out of season. I couldn't help wishing Kip was along.

"Isn't this wonderful! You feel so free out on the road," Gwen cried. "We could go anywhere. We could *disappear*."

"We don't have enough clothes along." I wondered if she'd brought extra money. "Anyway, we didn't tell Kip."

She made a dismissive noise.

"He's nice," she said thoughtfully, as if someone had questioned it—a funny thing to say about your husband. "But what's he in that dumb job at the courthouse for? He likes it that they vote him in, but of course they will, as long as he's a Democrat. And partly because he's good looking and smiles a lot. They may even vote for him partly because they know I'm sick! Why didn't he decide to do something interesting? He thinks he knows more than he does. Forrest and Clay"—his brothers, getting rich at their mill farther down the river—"they're nice, but what are they interested in except work and making money?"

When you begin to think how he is like the rest of his family, watch out. "You're crazy about him," I said lightly, to get her off this jag. Anyway, it had to be true; anyone would love Kip.

"When something like this hits you, you realize you've got just one life; till then you know it but don't *realize* it."

I felt sympathy, of course; of course I did. But she talked as if being sick had given her some superior wisdom; it had set her apart. (She was a little spoiled, my mother always said—the only child of aging parents.) And why had she picked him in the first place? We took getting married for granted, of course, it was simply what you did back then; but beyond that, why? Sex, I suppose, the need that draws men and women together—need overlooks so much. But I didn't want to look at that then, not *theirs*, I mean.

"You're getting better, you'll get your health back. Look, here's the South Carolina line."

I thought she'd want to turn back then, but, if anything, she stepped on the gas. Being in a new state made us farther away than ever. Were we ever going back?

We had lunch in a small-town hotel. There among the white cloths and quiet waiters, we were different; you might have thought we were two footloose girls off on a trip, going who knew where. We debated the choice of dessert, and took the banana pudding. Then she drove on. In another small town, she suddenly turned into the driveway of a big house with green striped awnings. "I've always wanted a house with awnings!" she said, turning the car around rather carelessly, and stopping. "You can drive now." I was relieved when, in late afternoon, I turned into the yard.

"We took a ride today," she said to Kip that night. "We drove down to South Carolina." Not quite challengingly.

"Oh! Well. Good. I hope you had fun." He looked not so much baffled as tired. He didn't ask who'd done the driving, or how far we went; he didn't ask one single thing.

I suppose she was getting worse. I suppose I was denying it, I suppose that's why I don't remember the specifics. I suppose.

She was using the cane he'd bought her, a handsome black one with a brass head; she visited the doctors in Charlotte from time to time, but medical science was not then what it is today, of course.

The night everything fell apart, we'd gone to a movie.

"I didn't like that movie," Gwen said on the way home. She didn't get out much, so she must have wanted the evening to be perfect. "Why'd we go to that movie?"

"It wasn't too bad, was it?" Kip said. "Lana Turner was very beautiful."

The wrong thing to say, maybe, considering Gwen's mood. We were passing some woods, and I said, "Hey, did you hear the owls last night?"

"Yeah, wonderful," Kip said.

"I didn't! I didn't hear them, why didn't you come tell me?" Gwen said in an anguished voice. Was she going to burst into tears? Kip patted her arm, and we were silent for a while.

Back at the house, some of their old college yearbooks were spread out in the living room. She'd been looking at them for a day or two, and after we settled down with some tea, she picked one of them up and riffled through it.

"Here's Jim Dellinger, remember him? I had quite a crush on him, and he finally asked me out. We went to a wonderful concert together. And a picnic—a wonderful picnic. And some other things."

"I guess that was before we got together, dearie," Kip said.

"Yes. You don't remember him at all? A good-looking guy, and not a bit stuck up. We went to *The Messiah* together at Christmas, it was so lovely, the choir in red robes—I was so moved, I nearly squeezed his hand to pieces. A swell guy."

"I'm sorry things didn't work out for you and Mr. Dellinger," Kip said, trying for lightness.

That would surely wake her up. But no. "Yes. If I'd married him. . . . Change one thing and everything else is different—isn't that true? I mean, think about it, how could it work any other way?"

It was stubborn of Kip to let a silence fall. I wanted to sink through the floor, I wanted to sneak out of the room. That was what I ought to have done, instead of saying, "It's not Kip's fault you're sick! You think it's easy for him?" It was automatic, like an in-law courtesy, taking up for the visitor.

Gwen turned a hollow look on me. "What do you know about it? Well. There's no love like your first love. Or is there? If I were a thousand miles away from here, I'd be well. I'd start over, nobody I knew, me and my cane, I swear I could make it, oh God." She wasn't crying, though. Hard as nails!

Something had touched Kip, and he went over and tried to put his arms around her. "It's all right, hon, you're going to be okay."

She got up and leaned on her cane; she was going to her room. "I can't stand it here any longer. I'm going to pray tonight that I die. I don't know what to pray for, for you two." She was balanced on the cane and starting for her room.

"Listen—" Kip moved along beside her. He followed her down the hall.

I couldn't read or look at picture books or anything else. I sat there, waiting for my heart to stop pounding.

Kip didn't return. I went to my room and got ready for bed, though it was early, thinking to read in bed. But after a while I couldn't stay there any longer, and I put on my robe and went down the hall, tiptoeing. I tiptoed to his room and tapped very lightly on his door.

I shouldn't have tiptoed. I shouldn't have tapped on his door.

He came to the door in his pajamas and said, "Wait a minute," but I stepped in, so she wouldn't hear us; I didn't want to disturb her, and that is true. I felt for her, I felt for her as much as I could in my young foolishness, but I felt for him too, and I stepped into his room while he was getting his bathrobe on, and said, "Kip, it's awful. I know she doesn't mean it. It's the disease." And I put my arms around him because I *felt* for him, and that's all. We held each other a while, we *needed* to, I think anyone could understand that. I don't suppose it was the only time we hugged. It's been a long time since then; I suppose there are things I've forgotten. Which is my privilege.

College catalogs came in the mail that spring. "Yes, I sent for them," Gwen said. She seemed to be in good spirits. "We can't have you wasting your life here. Pretty soon it'll be too late to ever go back."

Years later, I wondered what they said about me afterward. I think of her often now.

When Norris was sick for the last time, I wanted to say to the rest of the world: drop what you're doing, everybody, let the whole world get busy right now and keep this from happening! The doctors and nurses and friends and neighbors were resigned—how could that be? How could the postman come as usual, the people in cars drive past indifferently? A man was dying, about to be taken away for once and all. Call the authorities—this was our last chance, our final opportunity! For Norris, whom I hadn't always treasured.

That must have been what she felt, contemplating her own life.

Of course, Gwen didn't die young. Three or four years after I left, the disease went into remission. It was a long time before she went to a care center, and then it was because they couldn't get good help, my mother wrote.

"He wasn't a skirt chaser," Gwen said, "but he was drawn to women, it was just the way he was." She said it casually, with an easy, authoritative superiority.

I didn't want to talk about Kip. The past can almost startle me now; that's what time does. Kip: a nice guy, fascinating in my younger days; a guy I'd had a crush on. The morning after she'd been so angry and wanted to take her cane and leave, could I have said, "Nothing has ever happened between him and me, Gwen"? She might have said, "What on earth are you talking about?"—offended at the presumption, offended enough to change things between us forever. Which, to a great extent, happened anyway.

Here in the care center, she was looking good. Her face hadn't spread or gone puffy like so many of the faces around us. There was a little indentation in each cheek, as if the sculptor had pressed a fingertip there. She talked slowly, with an equanimity missing in the old days.

I'd been back before; I'd come back and hugged her and hugged Kip too; later I'd visited her after he was gone. Sometimes Norris was along on my visits, sometimes not. This was my first time back in some time. Norris had been poorly for years before he died, and I hadn't wanted to leave him alone out in California, the kids grown and gone.

"It was just the way Kip was. He *responded* to women," she said. "I wonder if people gossiped about him and some of the women that stayed with me." Was she asking me? People had been careful not to let anything slip to her, or else they'd hinted and she'd tuned them out. Then again, maybe nothing had happened, ever. I'd more or less refused to believe the gossip my mother reported about him and Ramelle Oliver. She wouldn't have been his type, with her showy sweetness, her plump legs in nurses' oxfords, her face going matronly early because of a budding double chin. The rumors made me almost angry.

"Two women and a man in a house—people gossip, they just will," I said. I wished that I could keep from wondering if she and Kip had gone on sleeping together during those years.

"He died right here, in the dining room."

"I know."

"I loved him, of course I loved him." Was she wrapping up the bothersome past in a neat package to file it away? "He did get on my nerves. Playing ping-pong out on the porch with whatever girl was there, kidding around, putting his arm around her shoulders—I was sensitive. Too sensitive." Was she remembering Ramelle, or me? "After all, I was sick! I felt *insecure*. I lived with uncertainty, whether I ought to have or not." A fretful look crossed her face; it was something she wanted to say, but not necessarily to me.

"I had a crush on him. A silly schoolgirl crush." Time to pull it all out in the open and get it over. Probably thinking about Kip all the time had had something to do with my marrying Norris as soon as I'd finished the next year at college.

"Did you!" Her manner was artificial and dismissive. Maybe with that illness you forgot things, though I'd never noticed it. More likely you harbored them. "Well, you weren't

the only one. . . . I wish Mal would stop by. Malcolm. I'd like
for you to meet him. We read poems to each other. Do you
remember 'The Night Has a Thousand Eyes'? Some of the
ones we used to love. 'Who Loves the Rain' . . . maybe they're
out of style, but I love them. I can imagine I'm fifteen again!"
She laughed.

"Wonderful. That's wonderful."

Mal didn't show up, though, and after a while I kissed
her goodbye. "Oh, Gwen, it's so great to see you. I wish
we hadn't lived so far apart, I've missed you so much!" I
was afraid tears would come to my eyes; really, I hadn't
let myself think, till I saw her again, how very much I *had*
missed her, how she appeared in all my memories of the
past, and in my dreams more nights than I could count.
She smiled politely, murmured, "I know." Without much
feeling, so far as I could tell.

It might have been something else, the illness, say, that
had thrown up this wall between her and me. And we were
so much alike!—two people who had felt our way through life
half-blindly, at the mercy of our dream worlds.

After people die, you think: I should have managed it
somehow. That is what you always think.

The past can be all squared away in your mind, too long ago
to think about at all, then something happens some gray day,
and everything falls into disorder, like a room shaken by an
earthquake. The books all in a heap on the floor, the china
jumbled and cracked in the cupboards.

Today there was a smell of ashes in the house: it rained all
week till today, and a little rain gets past the damper into the
fireplace. Gray outside, the smell of ashes indoors. And my
second narrow escape today came as I walked by the river, a

river smaller than the one of my youth, but big enough. I was walking the dog, and the river tempted me terribly, flowing by so close. I'd sink like a lump of lead, and never think about any of this again. (Never again be old, living alone, either.) But there was Riley, old Riley, slouching along ahead of me, his old doggy, black and tan hips shaking. What would I do, let go the leash and leave him on his own? I'd never do that. He counts on me, he's expecting me to be here dishing up his supper and patting his head from here on out.

You're depressed, my daughter says, go to the doctor. I tell her I don't want to get started on pills. Will a pill tell me I wasn't a fool back then? I wouldn't take its word for anything. Soon there'll be a sunny morning when I can put it aside, when I can see how long ago it was and how little it should have mattered in the end. I have been through this before now, and it's passed.

There are the memories from earlier times, of course; they are what I should think of. The August night of a Perseid shower when we lay on quilts spread on the grass in her backyard and watched the stars fall. They fell almost continuously: "Look, look, there's another!" For us back then the stars were not masses of ionized gas whirling in fiery turbulence, but beautiful fixed points that once in a while lost their moorings in the heavens and streaked down the sky.

Our fathers stand by the pump house, talking, their heads cocked toward the sky. Our mothers move around inside the lighted house, talking as they tidy up the kitchen. Soon they will come out and lie down on a quilt too. The cats, who live outdoors, will walk around and over us, purring. The stars will go on falling all night, and we will sleep there together, at peace, our lives, fresh and barely used, still before us.

MIAMI, 1959

The people in the establishment at Forty Mile Bend called her after ten that night, and told her he was there. He was sleeping in the back room, but they were going to close up before too long, and somebody better come get him. "Thought maybe he'd just had one too many, to tell you the truth, but I'm thinking now he might be sick." They halfway knew him—her husband, Dexter; he passed that way every so often. He and his partner made air boats for use in the Everglades.

She was sweating as she dialed her daughter's number; she felt the dampness on her upper lip and under her breasts. "Honey? Is Gary still up?"

"No, he's gone to bed. Why, what you want with him?"

"I've got to go pick up your dad. He's sick, up at Forty Mile Bend, they called me. Somebody's got to drive his car back. I—"

"Brock's still up, he's got his license now, he sits up half the night anyhow—" Her voice faded as she called across the room. "Sure, Brock'll go."

There wasn't time to change from the tent dress she wore around the house, but at her bureau she lifted the dress and flipped some bath powder from the big puff onto her body; she stepped from her house scuffs into some shoes, got her purse, and left the house. Outside the night air was warm and moist; she fancied there was a faint evil smell, as if something was burning far out in the Everglades. Out on the Trail, the road would be dark and empty, the headlights picking up nothing but the highway, or once in a great while, some animal, maybe an armadillo, that you wished to God wasn't there in the road.

Brock, her grandson, was not at all sorry to hop in the car and sit beside her in the sedan as they rocketed out toward the Tamiami Trail. A little later, when they were out of the city, she might let him drive. His mother, in her eternal terry cloth scuffs, had followed him out to the car over the damp grass, reminding him not to speed. His grandmother might want to nod off, though, and he'd be on his own. Farther on, alongside the road, there were ditches full of dark water.

He regarded his grandparents with a kind of sympathetic amusement, or perhaps it was a loving pity. In his mind he called them Dexter and Faye. His grandmother, hauling her heavy haunches into a car and making it sink an inch or two lower; his grandfather, downtown at the courthouse in his monkey suit. In the family everyone said, "He works *at the courthouse*," not "He's an elevator operator." He'd retired from that now, and made air boats. He went hunting in the Everglades; his grandmother cooked venison and even weirder stuff.

He hoped his grandmother wasn't going to bring up his uncle again. Whenever his grandfather did anything out of the way, someone would say, in an almost reverent tone, "He's never been the same after what happened to Brock." Brock, his uncle, the one he was named for, had been taking flying lessons, and was doing "real well," they all said, but something happened one day when he was coming in for a landing. The crash left him in pieces; his father, waiting there at the airport, had run around collecting the parts lying on the ground, reassembling Brock—here's an arm, there's a foot; they could hardly pull him away and get him home. Brock the younger hated the story; it was sad, it was grisly, and his own name was in it.

But his grandmother didn't mention his uncle tonight. She was driving, that was all she was doing, making a bee-line for Forty Mile Bend. "You've got a lead foot, Gramma, you know that? You're over the speed limit right now."

"Yeah, well, those folks want to close up some time. And he's sick, we've got to get on up there. Better I get a ticket than you. You'll be driving his car back, all the way, all by your lonesome."

The cot where he slept was in the back room, a cramped storeroom; shelves he could have reached out and touched held boxes and crates, bottles full and empty, an old folded-up jacket. He was snoring lightly, his forehead shiny with sweat.

She seized his arm. "Deck, Deck, wake up! Gotta go home! Wake up!"

Beside her, Brock leaned over and shook him. He was a slim boy, but tall; she hoped he was stronger than he looked. He'd become not only taller but quieter and farther away in the last year or two, with an expression that hung between smiling and not smiling, sometimes turning into a crooked smile that might be holding back amusement.

Dexter opened his eyes and looked at them wildly. His eyes closed again. He smelled sweaty, but not boozy. "Let's get him up. Wake up!" she screamed, startling Brock.

The man waiting behind them said, "I'll hep you," and she edged away, making herself smaller. Brock and the man had him sit on the edge of the cot for a moment; he stared blankly, but moved along in their grip when they got him up.

Out in his car was his blue sweater, a sweater that had been missing for at least a year; she saw it as they passed his car. "Where on earth. . . ." She held the door to her car open while the men got him onto the back seat. "Oh, the keys, feel in his pockets. O.K., I'll see you back at my house, honey. You can keep the car till tomorrow, I don't want to drive you home tonight."

Was it only his imagination that the car smelled perfumed? On impulse he picked up the sweater there in the passenger seat; it had a sweetish smell, like his mother's dresser drawers.

He'd heard snatches of what they said about ol' Dexter, his mother murmuring over the phone to his grandmother. *Tomcatting*—that was the expression. Maybe the old man had been tomcatting around. Would too much sex make you like he was right now? Close up, he'd smelled sweaty, but there'd also been a trace of cologne or aftershave—getting ready for somebody, fixing himself up?

His grandmother was getting settled in the other car; he was going to follow her, worse luck—no chance to open up out on the road. He opened the glove compartment; maybe looking for a flashlight—or something; maybe for women's panties. There was something funny there, all right: a pack of condoms. Oh, man. He slipped them into his pocket. Wouldn't do for her to find them. He himself wouldn't have any use for them right away, but you never knew, did you, ha ha. He didn't mind thinking about condoms, but—your *grandfather*? The thrill of the knowledge faded, and he wanted to give it back.

His grandmother was pulling out, leaving this little oasis of gas pumps and bright lights in the dark, flat landscape, and he pulled out after her. Thank God she was the one carrying Grandpop—but what if he suddenly waked up in the back seat and did something to startle her?

Back at home, the old man opened his eyes as soon as they touched him. He groaned. But in a moment he sat up and began to inch along the seat toward the car door where his wife waited. He was groaning. "Oh Jesus. Oh God. Oh Faye!"

She'd forgotten to leave the porch light on, but there were lights on inside the house; they eased him up the steps. In the living room they stopped to rest; she was puffing. "Oh, Lord. And I'm working tomorrow," she muttered. She still worked part-time as a checker at the nearest supermarket; she could ring the stuff up really fast, her eyes occasionally going to the customer's face as she made a little effortless chit-chat.

They let him down on the side of the bed; she peeled the cover back around him, and he flopped down full length. She stood, surveying him. "Thanks, old girl," he muttered, reaching toward her without connecting. He opened his eyes wider and turned toward her a smile beautiful with relief. "Oh, God." His gaze took in Brock. "Thanks, sonny."

Brock took the old man's shoes off. "Anything else?"

"No, that's good enough, go on home to bed." She was pulling the old man's pants off with a great tug, exposing his white undershorts and his skinny white legs and their knotty veins. "That's good enough, you can sleep like that. . . . Next time I'm going to just leave you up there, hear?" She whacked his thigh, but she was smiling. She looked more rested than when they'd set out. She went around to the other side of the bed and plopped down, sagging the mattress, kicking off her shoes. (Was she going to sleep in her dress?) "Turn off the light, honey, and lock the door as you go out." His grandfather was already reaching out toward her.

He drove away, happy to be out late, with wheels, even if it was his grandfather's aging Buick. Wheels were what he needed, to speed off into the future, away from his brothers and sisters, away from Dad the Plumber. His grandparents had been, off and on, a kind of refuge from home, but now he was glad to get away from them; at the moment he felt for them a kind of sorrowful contempt. He wasn't planning to get old, and if and when he did, it wouldn't be like that, it would be an altogether more elegant undertaking. He considered driving all the way to his girlfriend's house in a nicer part of town, honking as he passed, then gave up the idea. It was really a waste, being out so late with wheels and nothing to do. He headed for the nearest Steak 'n Shake and went inside; he could at least have a bite and see who else was up at this hour.

That sweater in the car! The old man had been somewhere he'd been before—and he imagined a woman, a woman he visited up the road every so often. Somebody slim, in high heels, a little worn with experience, maybe blonde, eyes darkened with a bit too much stuff on the lashes, a little *cheap*, as his mother would have said. He imagined them kissing at the door, a long clench, then moving together, like a couple dancing, toward the bedroom. Taking off their clothes. . . . His grandfather had left the picture; it had become his own fantasy.

At home there was really no safe place to keep the condoms, otherwise he might have kept them for the sheer sophistication of it. Leaving the Steak 'n Shake, he threw the packet into the darkness at the edge of the parking lot.

His grandparents, now—her flopping down into bed; his reaching out for her—embarrassing. What held them together? The old pain of his uncle's falling out of the sky and ending up in pieces? All those years, all those homely years?

He'd turned toward an unfamiliar part of town. It gave him pleasure to drive past houses he'd never seen before; it was almost like being in a new town. He would live in one of these unfamiliar, more expensive parts of town some day. Many of the houses were dark now, only a dim light burning in the back or in an upstairs hall. He felt the pleasure of being up later than the people in them; it was almost like possessing superior knowledge.

His grandparents, that disheveled old couple lying in bed, lingered in his thoughts, like a problem he hadn't solved. The old man ought not to be running around, of course; crazy, at his age. And her—she ought to kick him out. Awkward, though, him moving out, dividing stuff up. She'd probably be afraid at night, by herself. Still, that was what she ought to do. He might tell his mother this. No, better stay off the subject.

He turned toward home. There he coasted into the driveway and parked behind the family car under the carport. A dim light burned in the living room. His mother would stick her head out of the bedroom and ask, "You get him?" "Yeah, he's O.K., we got him," he'd say, and head for the room where his younger brother snored lightly and perhaps murmured in sleep. A pity he didn't have his own room, with some place to hide those condoms, just for the hell of it.

Some time—he'd be away from it all some time. Some time, some time, he thought, taking the key from under the flower pot to unlock the front door. Some time.

For a long time after her son died, Faye had talked to him in thought at bedtime, rounding up the events of the day, which, up in heaven, he knew all about, of course. But the habit had faded; the past was wrapped up and put away.

Now, lying in bed, she was still savoring the sweetness of relief. In the car coming back, hearing his snores, she'd remembered his father's stroke, when she and Deck were young and living with his parents. His father's stertorous breathing that day! This might be it, he might never get out of the car again. But he had come back to life. It would happen some time, the terrible thing, but she wasn't going to think of *some time*. You feared it, it didn't happen, and then you could go back to believing it never would.

In the living room the mantel clock bonged the hour. She told it to be quiet. Sure, time was passing, but never mind. Let things stay like this; now was good enough. Let it be forever now.

Deck was snoring. She poked him. "Turn over!" She moved closer to him and put her arm lightly across his body. It was somewhat uncomfortable, but she left it there till sleep overcame her.

THE END OF A GOOD PARTY

Reine, my wife, was never in a hurry to go to the parties in the Grove. She'd claim to have trouble getting a sitter, or she'd say it was a long way to Coconut Grove from Hialeah, and it was, of course, in more ways than one. Back then, the time I'm talking about, the papers already called Hialeah "a largely blue-collar community," as if these endless streets of pastel, tile-roofed houses were all that different from a lot of Miami. Our street is unusual; it has a row of Australian pines down a center parkway. The pines are dear to Reine.

I thought her foot-dragging came mostly from the grudging way some wives look at their husband's old friends, as if everything has to start with them. My first wife wasn't crazy about the Grove crowd either, but then she was a cute little airhead. Whenever Julian appeared at the back porch jalousies crying, "Hast seen the White Whale?" she didn't know what he was talking about. Reine knows, though she's not intellectual like the Grove people; she always knows more than I expect. She's actively quiet, like someone who's secretly memorizing the conversation or taking notes. I fell in love with her long black hair, which used to hang below her shoulders; now she works it into various shapes.

Some Saturday nights she'd line up a sitter and we'd head for the Grove. It wasn't yuppie yet, or plastered with umpteen signs of security systems; it was overgrown and beautiful, the way it still is, the stop streets hazardous with foliage, even in the part that wasn't so fancy, the part where we were headed. The bohemian part, you might call it. Sometimes it seemed to smell like ripe mangoes or exotic vegetation, plants that might bloom at night once in a great while.

I admit it—sometimes I drank too much at those parties. I was having a good time, and I got sloshed. I may have made a few passes, and I regret any pain this may have caused Reine. Maybe that's what happened the night she went over to the police station and told them I was drunk.

She came back with a cop, who stood around embarrassed and uncertain. Someone turned off the music. "Everything O.K. here? The lady says you're intoxicated. Any disorderly conduct? Any altercations, verbal or otherwise?" Incredulous looks around the room, smiles and frowns.

"O.K.," the cop said. "You drive?" he asked Reine. "When you start home, now, don't let him drive if there's any doubt in your mind. You do the driving, O.K.? Have a safe evening," and he got away. A long silence as he started the police car out in the yard.

Reine was torn between the wish to ditch me and go home (where her younger sister would be in a deep sleep on the couch, and had probably forgotten to wake little Teddy for the late-night trip to the bathroom) and the need to stay and keep up her surveillance. The talk was stirring again; someone turned the music back on. Reine sat down in a chair and closed her eyes, and all at once I was afraid she might do something drastic, like cry.

"Hey," Guy said, "Reine's tired, why don't you take her home." It sounded casual and kindly, and he and Sheila started dancing again.

We started off; I fell asleep in a few minutes. Then Reine was outside the car, opening my door and poking me. "Wake up, help me!" We were stopped in front of a big house in Coral Gables, where there was stuff piled on the curb for the trash truck. She was pulling carpeting off the pile and stuffing it into the trunk. "It's perfectly good, I'll shampoo it. There's enough here for the back room." People did that—scavenged in the rich neighborhoods. The idea never appealed to me.

"Couldn't I just give blood instead?" But I got out and tried to help. There was a pile of floor cushions there too, and she grabbed a couple of those and flung them into the back seat before we took off again.

Julian wasn't at that party; that was after he was gone, permanently gone. First he'd been away temporarily, teaching high school in Wyoming; the fact that it was the West gave it the necessary romantic touch. Before that, when he was still in town, working at his dad's tire company, we'd hang out together some afternoons; we were pals from high school. If I was working the night shift, I'd take a pill to stay awake, and we'd go call on somebody. A lot of the Grove people worked at home, or if they taught they'd be home in the summer.

They painted pictures or wrote book reviews or columns for the paper; actually I never understood what some of them did. We might go see Sheila. She lived with her folks, she and her little boy. She'd been mixed up with a Basque jai alai player and he'd married her, but he went off to play somewhere else and never came back.

She'd be reading some big book, and Julian would say, "What deathless masterpiece of world literature is engrossing you now, my dear?" He could say stuff like that; he had a deep grin that said something funnier was dancing around in his mind. He was gangly, with large, squarish teeth, and long feet in black shoes. All his early occupations had been jokes. In the Army, he wouldn't stop picking up litter when his detail was over; he'd be out on the grounds alone as night came on, spearing nearly invisible bits of gum wrapper with his pointed stick, and he addressed his superior officer as "mon capitaine." After they discharged him, he went to the police academy, and later you'd see him directing traffic downtown with elaborate, Chaplinesque gestures. "Does he want to wear a uniform," Guy asked," "or hold all uniforms up to scorn?" He never told us. After the police department let him go, he went back to school for a little while, then went out West to teach.

When he got sick, he came back to Miami and consulted his old friend Elliott. When he got worse and Elliott couldn't doctor him anymore, Elliott doctored the lung X-rays. "See? It's shrinking, see that? We're gettin' there, we're gettin' there," putting on a fake Southern accent to show good cheer. Elliott told us this later at a party; he and his wife came to one occasionally, though mostly he'd left the Grove crowd behind—he had a busy practice, and a house down in South Dade with a pool and colored lights hidden in the shrubs around the front door.

Julian might not have been fooled by the X-rays. He was feeling low. He came to parties, but he was ill, ill and subdued. We sat together on somebody's front steps on the Fourth of July, the party going on in the house and yard behind us, and he said, "What can you do on the Fourth of July but set yourself ablaze and jump from the fifth story singing 'There's a Star-spangled Banner Waving Somewhere'?" I laughed, but I didn't know how to take it. It worried me. We went back in to the party. When he left, there was a lull in the talk, like a moment of silence.

At the memorial service for Julian in the Unitarian Church, I didn't get up and say anything; I let others do it. I thought about the afternoons on the jalousied porch at Sheila's, Julian and Sheila talking about what she was reading, maybe Marcel Proust, a French writer; out in the yard her little boy would be swinging and swinging with a dreamy look on his face, his lips moving as if he were singing. Sitting with them, I always felt a deep contentment that seemed to sing along with him—as if this was where I belonged. As if I were settled at home and would stay there from then on.

The summer I'm thinking about was the summer the musicians from the Islands came to Miami with their steel drums and calypso songs. They performed at the Sir John and the Mary Elizabeth, two hotels in colored town, as it was called. The black people let us come and listen, they sang about how it was love, love, love alone that caused King Edward to leave his throne. A few of the musicians came to some of the Grove parties, and Sheila's little sister had a terrible crush on a tall black guy named Joshua; during the parties she'd often be sitting with him in a car out in the yard, holding hands and kissing. Some of the parties went on very late, and I'd pass around the stay-awake pills I had for shift work at the power company. Sometimes we'd go to breakfast down at the Holsum Bakery in South Miami, the only place anywhere nearby that was open at 4 a.m.

It was the summer after Julian died, and at a party one night Claudia said, "Let's have a séance. Let's get in touch with Julian!" She had a hoarse, rich voice.

"You know about séances?" Reuel asked.

"I know enough, I know the basic premise."

She led us into another room away from most of the party. I suppose you'd call her a forceful personality. I remember hearing her across the room once, exclaiming, "You don't have the *right* not to like Goya!" I loved it when they got worked up about stuff like that. Claudia had an abandon that could sweep you along—*why quibble, let's do it.* She had a full figure and a full mouth, and high-colored cheeks, and clothes that looked like something she'd thought up and put together. She'd married a fellow from Spain and she'd wanted him to be a bullfighter, but apparently in Spain that occupation is not really upper-class, more like being a baseball player, and he had no interest in it. Anyway, pretty soon he was busy fighting some disease instead—something went wrong with his liver or kidneys, and in a couple of years he was dead. She went to Mexico, like a lot of artists, and got mixed up with a rich married man, people said, and had a child. Later she heard he was going to snatch the little girl, and she left in a hurry. Why did she do those crazy things? Some notion of *living*, I guess. Because they were there for the doing.

We found a card table, and the four of us sat down at it. Reuel, perfect as always in his open button-down collar, was there out of curiosity, to see what Claudia would cook up; Libby was there because she wasn't much of a dancer or even much of a talker, and got bored early. I thought they might not be the right people for this. If there were any.

"We need a control," Claudia said. "It's somebody who's been dead quite a while, usually."

Reuel laughed. "Yeah, somebody who knows the ropes over there on the other side."

She turned out the lamp, and someone closed the door; there was only a crack of light showing under it. There was no fan in the room, and it felt warm and close.

"My grandmother—my grandmother Batterman. I never knew her, but I'm like her. She'll be my control. Ready? All right, eyes closed. Very quiet."

We closed our eyes, and Claudia called in a firm voice, "Grandmother! Grandmother Mary Matilda Batterman of Brown's Summit, do you hear me? Grandmother, it's Claudia. Are you there?"

It was silly, but it gave me goose pimples anyway, and I jiggled the table with my knee.

"Vic, stop it! I'm serious."

"Sorry, sorry! Go ahead. I'm sorry!"

"Grandmother, Grandmother Mary Matilda, are you there?"

We waited; nothing happened. "I can't reach her," Claudia said, as surprised and perturbed as if she had done this a dozen times and it usually worked. "I need a different control."

"Chief Osceola," I said. I said it without thinking: the name had come from out of the blue, quick as an arrow.

"Chief Osceola of the Seminole Tribe," Claudia called, "do you hear me? Are you there? Chief Osceola! We want to reach Julian Rosemond."

But nothing happened, and Claudia said, "We'll do it without a control. Think of Julian! Join hands. Think of him."

Her hand was warm in mine, and I knew mine in hers would feel hard and calloused. Reuel had my other hand. I thought hard about Julian, and I saw him in a sixth-grade classroom, writing something on the board, mountains showing beyond the window. I could imagine he was still alive, far away. I heard him talking in that joke way: "Surely you jest"—something he liked to say. Julian, Julian, surely you jest, pretending you're gone! There're things I've been saving to tell you.

Claudia murmured, "Julian, Julian! We miss you." We sat on for another couple of minutes, and then Reuel said, "Well, we tried," and got up and turned on the lamp.

I looked at Claudia and squeezed her hand. "You were good, dearie. Thanks." I thought tears might be glistening in her eyes. "I think we reached him. That was him, telling me to try Chief Osceola. It really was."

"I know." She squeezed my hand.

A car engine started out in the yard; people were beginning to leave. Sheila's little sister came in from outside, flushed and dreamy from necking with the Islands musician.

Claudia was getting her purse. "Let's go." Outside in the yard someone was singing a calypso we'd heard at the Sir John. The man tells the woman, stay home and mind baby. That's all he says, *Brown-skinned girl, stay home and mind baby, Brown-skinned girl, stay home and mind baby. . . . And if I don't come back—stay home and mind baby!* It was a simple little tune, tender and melancholy.

I followed Claudia to her apartment in an old frame fourplex near the downtown Grove. There was a teasing little breeze from the bay, and the feel of the water nearby. We went upstairs and sat on her studio couch.

That make-believe séance had made me kind of gloomy. "I had the feeling we were so close and yet so far, y'know?"

"No, no. Think how wonderful it was! He spoke to you."

If he did. But I loved her trying to convince me.

That feeling with women!—it's different with each one. That quick, easy electricity that pulsed between me and my first wife, the sleazy little creature with ankle-strap shoes and tops that were always pulling up and showing her bare midriff—that was different from this. There was something languorous and soothing about our kisses, Claudia's and mine. We were more like an old married couple, home from the party, rather drunk, routinely, gently amorous. I felt at home there in that conglomeration of rooms with uneven floors and doors painted different colors, and pictures, hers and other people's, and vines growing in old Chianti bottles.

"What if she wakes up?" I whispered as we went into the bedroom. The little girl was six or seven.

"She never does." But she fastened the gate-hook on the door. We helped each other undress. That ordinary plump body—how I wanted to bury myself in it, over in the half-made bed! My God, I couldn't believe this. "A Consummation devoutly to be wished," Julian used to quote. From Shakespeare. A Consummation devoutly to be wished.

I thought about it a lot afterwards. There was a run of Saturday nights, and some other nights too, when I sat at home thinking, and it didn't make me happy. I sat out on the front stoop and smoked and wondered about that night with Claudia. And tonight: were they partying without me down in the Grove? This stayed on my mind.

Was I supposed to have called her next day from the corner drugstore? People can hold all sorts of things against you. People can change their minds about things and remember them wrong. Things can get all mixed up.

There was plenty of regular life going on around me, of course. The ice cream truck's bell tinkled and the kids ran out, and when my little girl Melanie dropped her Screwball, which is basically purple ice, and got dirt in it, I ran after the truck for a replacement. The kids played in our yard or the one next door, threatening each other with squirts from the hose and chasing lightning bugs.

They went inside, and I sat on the front stoop, smoking, and maybe watched a plane coming in low toward the airport, its winking lights disappearing behind the Australian pines. I saw my crowd dancing late in the evening, Claudia barefoot, wearing her India-print-bedspread dress. Guy slightly drunk, a patch of sweat showing on the back of his shirt. It felt like a long time since anyone had called me about a party.

If Julian had been around, we'd have hopped into his faded black sedan and gone down to check it out. But he wasn't around, and I stayed there on the stoop and watched the Florida sky grow pale, the faint blue lingering over the tops of the pines as twilight came on.

That night at Claudia's, I woke up as the first morning coolness came in the window. The electric fan across the room was still on. The blinds were open for the breeze, and pretty soon I could make out the pictures on the wall. I got up and dressed without making any noise. I was slightly hung over, and very happy. The song somebody had been singing as the party broke up played in my head on the way home. *And if I don't come back*—but there was never any question of my not coming back. And if I felt too much at home in the Grove, it was nobody's fault but mine. It had happened, that's all; I couldn't do anything about it. It was the way it was.

If some great Parent who couldn't be denied, my mother down from heaven, or the Holy Father himself, came and said, "You have been unfaithful to sweet Reine, the mother of your children—say you're sorry," I wouldn't have been able to. To Reine I could say truthfully: It wasn't *her*, exactly; I didn't love her in a way that you'd understand, and she didn't love me. It mattered in a way that's hard to explain.

How long did I worry? Two months? Two and a half?

It felt longer. It felt like a long sleep. Hibernation in Hialeah.

I woke up in the fall. Somebody who'd been away for a while came back to town; there was a party, and they called me. I saw it was crazy to think that something as meaningless as that night at Claudia's would change anything. Things were pretty much the way they'd been. The musicians had gone back to the Islands, though, and fall was coming. A few leaves had drifted onto the median beneath the banyans on Coral Way.

It wasn't the last Grove party I went to, but it stays in my mind as if it had been. As if I already knew then that Guy and Winifred would split up, and a few years later,

Reuel and Diane. As if I already knew that Reuel would move to New York and Diane would be begging over on the Beach, by choice, people said. (I never went over there to see her; who'd want to see her begging?) Claudia went north in a few years to live with an elderly aunt; she had no pension and not much Social Security. Later she took a job as a housekeeper for a priest. She'd talked theology for years—Teilhard de Chardin, I guess he was theology. (Me, I just took the kids to church.) But she kept house for the priest, and after a while they lived together. "Making her peace with the church at least," Guy said. "In her own way." I pictured her living in some old-fashioned red brick rectory, fixing healthful dishes with sprouts and tofu. I wasn't mooning over her, just thinking about her. I didn't love her much more than I loved Winifred or Diane, or Sheila, who was dead.

These people who've moved away—mostly they don't have family left here, so if they pass on, their obits probably won't be in the *Herald*. Any time could be obits time: Sheila died young, not even sixty. We smoked, including some pot now and then; we drank and took pills, what do you expect? But I don't want to see the obits if they come before mine. You know that feeling of relief people are supposed to have reading them, that it's somebody else and not them? I don't believe I'd feel that at all.

In my mind I go back to that last party, the sound of car doors slamming out in the yard as people begin to leave; myself, probably kind of sloshed, my arms around Guy and Sheila as they danced, the three of us dancing around together for a minute. That's what I go back to, that moment at the end of a good party. Things winding down, but not for keeps, you know; not forever.

THE NEXT TO LAST LINE

It was their second conference, and they had gone through the preliminary pleasantries. Bettina Thayer was shuffling through the two or three pages that held his poems (gathering ammunition, he thought, being convinced that she wasn't much interested in his work, which he thought of as his *kind* of poem). She'd moved her chair away from the desk, off to the side, and they sat close together in the long, narrow office with the half-empty bookshelves.

"Maybe you should try shrinking this longest one, I think there's some deadwood in there. And I marked the fourth stanza, there's something a little off in the syntax, I think you ought to straighten that out. Maybe try thinking of it as prose." She studied the pages again. "Once in a while the meter gets kind of jog-trot, I'd say roughen it up a little. Well, that's some stuff for you to think about, anyway," while he nodded, distracted by stray thoughts, as usual in her presence. How old was she?—thirty-five to his thirty? Her gleaming brown hair, parted in the middle, swung down toward her face, and she pushed it behind her ears. How could she bear doing that over and over?—it was almost a tic. She had a sweet smile, her eyelids slightly lowered in a conspiratorial way.

She asked what he was reading ("a little of this, a little of that," unwilling to say that at the moment it was mostly Dick Francis), then asked, "Have you worked any more on that short poem I liked?"

"'The Beach House'? No—I've been thinking about it. You know how you think about things at odd moments, you have your best thoughts when you're just walking along or in the shower? That was the thing about newspaper work—sometimes a week later I'd think how I ought to have described the guy I interviewed." Wondering if she remembered that he'd worked on a paper for a couple of years; probably she didn't bother storing up such facts. That almost excessive sweetness might be cover for a lack of complete attentiveness.

"Oh, yes. Oh yes. Well—one line of that poem really stuck in my mind, Sean, that next to last line. I liked it so much—well, in fact, I borrowed it and put it in a poem. I hope you're flattered."

"Well! I suppose. But where does that leave my poem?"

She seemed surprised at the question. She shifted in her chair, straightening her skirt, pulling it a little closer to her knees.

"I know—I can't just take your line. Well—if I dedicated the poem to you, how about that?"

"Um-m—I don't know. Well, let me think about it."

She turned through the papers in her hands, and made a few more comments that he barely took in. Appropriating that line!—what a nerve.

When he got up to leave, she said, with her always-warm smile, "Don't forget, I'm having that little gathering Friday night."

"I hadn't forgotten. Well, I can't quite make up my mind about that line you want."

"Oh." She was still surprised. "Well, think about it, please."

He didn't know the town well, only the downtown and, close to it, the neighborhood of his apartment building. Bettina Thayer's house was farther out, in a neighborhood of ordinary two-story frame houses, old-fashioned, respectable and unattractive. He had trouble making out the house numbers, but on his second pass through the block he recognized some classmates inside a small, brightly lighted house. It was a little box someone had found for her to rent; the entrance had a funny little curved roof, like a tilde. He had to park some distance away and walk back. There were piles of leaves still waiting for pick-up by the curb, and a few leaves whirled in the updraft from passing cars.

His classmates looked captive, crowded together in Bettina Thayer's miniature living room. Three of them were packed in tight on the sofa—Annie of the severely short haircut and the teeny gold earrings, chubby Justine with the blinding red lipstick, and big, bearded Ruxton; the others were scattered around in a loose semicircle. Bettina Thayer, tall and graceful in heels, was moving around, tucking her hair behind her ears, inviting them into the next room, where the wine and food were set out, and after a while the living room gridlock eased.

Bettina was talking about California when he went into the next room, which had dull brown cabinets around the wall, with a round dining table in the middle. "Yes, I've felt more Californian than ever since I've been in the Midwest, absolutely."

"Oh, the poor old Midwest, everybody's always beating up on it," somebody said.

"You were born during an earthquake, that makes you a true, full-blooded Californian," Sean said. He had come across this fact in an interview with her in an obscure magazine, and he felt superior in the possession of it.

She laughed. "Well, sort of. It was just the mildest temblor—it just rattled the oven rack, my grandmother said. My mother thought it was part of the process." She didn't seem at all surprised that he knew of it.

Back in the living room, Charlie and Justine were talking about magazines. "How many times do you send to one if they keep rejecting you?"

"Actually I never thought about it," Charlie said. "Most of them reject me, so I can't get too choosey. Why, do you?"

"Three rejections and they're off my list of places," Justine said firmly. "Of course, I've been lucky lately. Do you keep sending places where they turn you down a lot, Sean?"

"What makes you think there're such places?" He laughed. "Depends on the rejection slip. If they bother to scrawl 'Thanks' or 'Sorry,' I give them another chance. But you've got to have a tough hide in this business."

Over at the sofa, Annie was holding up a new book from the coffee table. She called to Bettina, in the doorway, "Do you like this woman's stuff?"

"Well—she's sort of a friend of mine. So I sort of have to. Actually I like some of it quite a lot."

"Oh," Annie said, clearly disappointed. She put the book back and put another book on top of it.

Tyler sat down beside her and picked up a book, a new novel. "This guy—I dated his daughter once. . . . He's sure won a lot of prizes." He stared at the picture on the dust jacket. "He looks furtive, doesn't he?"

"You'd look furtive too if you imagined all the crap he dreams up."

"His daughter—oh, man, she was a piece of work. A piece of work!"

Nearby, Michelle had corralled Ruxton. Sean had written in his journal: "Michelle: talking to her is like panning for gold: you have to go through a ton of dreck to get a few worthwhile nuggets." (A little pretentious; he'd been flexing his writing muscles.) She was good-natured and rather pretty in a wraith-like way; she must have been anorexic once, to be so thin, and he couldn't help wondering what her tiny breasts must be like under the loose little top—probably rudimentary little knobs. She was talking about her landlord. "He roots through the garbage, looking for bottles and cans he can turn in?—for a nickel a throw? They say in the spring when people move out and leave their cast-offs on the curb he's out there gathering up stuff to furnish his apartments with—oh, he is something."

"But that's good, digging out the cans and bottles, it's recycling—what's wrong with that?" Ruxton said. "The furniture too, what the hell, why take it to the dump if it's still good? People throw away a lot of good stuff."

Once Sean had tried to do a poem about these people. *Afternoons in the movie house, alone—*(Annie). *At fifty, on the podium at last / He reads too long* (Charlie). But it was too hard, and he'd sensed a kind of buried arrogance in it.

What would they say about him? Older than the others, maybe a little stand-offish; well-read ("and he lets you know it"?). Tonight, wearing a good jacket. ("Not a bad-looking guy"?) He gave a mental shrug. Annie got up from the sofa and came to talk to him. ("Basically sympathetic"?)

People were beginning to leave. He was going to linger and deal with the business of that line she'd lifted. Lifted, appropriated, purloined, abstracted, took, stole. Borrowed, she called it, but how could it be borrowed, with no chance of a payback? He imagined, at the foot of the poem, the words *for Sean Smith.* Would that be enough? Ever since she'd spoken of it, the line had rung in his mind. Certainly it was a good line; he might bring the rest of that poem up to it, and have a winner. Something that would appear in a good magazine, and then in anthologies. His first book: *The Beach House and Other Poems.*

Not too likely. Still. He went to the kitchen and poured the last of the red wine into his glass.

It turned out to be easy to linger. The last people to leave were a couple he didn't know well, and they didn't wait for him to go with them. He was able to say, "Let's talk it over, shall we?"

"Of course." She sank onto the sofa. "Sit down." She kicked off her shoes. "Do you like my shoes?"

"Oh, yes, they're great, I noticed them before."

"They cost more than everything else I have on put together, isn't that amazing?" Her arm lay across the back of the sofa, reaching toward him.

"Well, about that line. This is something new in my experience. And I suppose in yours too. So I've had a hard time with it, really. Maybe dedicating the poem to me would do. Maybe I'd rather you just didn't use it." He touched her arm lightly, to soften the words. He'd have liked the world to know she admired the line that much, but she was unlikely to give him full credit.

"Sean—forgive me. I've got a confession to make. I sent that poem out as soon as I finished it. Of course the magazine might not take it."

He heard his voice rising. "Are you kidding? Even if it weren't any good"—he pulled himself back a little—"even if it's not up to your usual, they'd probably buy it, that's how this business works. You're 'hot,' read the blurbs on the back of your last book. 'This book shows she is a force to be reckoned with in American poetry.' Big names on the back. They'll buy the poem, the odds are ninety to one."

"Maybe," she said softly. She touched his shoulder. "I'm sorry. If they take it, I'll add the dedication to you."

He was trying to think. "How about—how about a simple footnote for that line. 'This line is from Sean Smith.' That's the most honest way to do it, isn't it? Or take the line out. Make up another line, a substitute, it wouldn't be that hard for you."

She got up suddenly. "Hey. Maybe if you read my poem and see how I've used it, you'd feel better about it—I'll show you a copy."

"Don't bother. If you're saying you can use my line better than I can, that's insulting."

She sank down again. "Oh, God. I'm so sorry, forgive me. I didn't mean that, of course, not at all. I have respect for your talent." She showed a sorrowful face.

He took her hand. "Listen, I'm sorry to get so wound up about it, but it bothers me. If you weren't so nice and, I might add, so attractive, I wouldn't for one minute be considering letting you have it at all." Was he a little drunk, on three glasses of wine? He'd gone too far; he'd crossed the border into a place it might be hard to pull back from, a place where embarrassment lay in store for him.

But she squeezed his hand. "I do understand how you feel. But I love that line. I love it as much as if I'd written it myself. As someone I lived with used to say."

"Oh, yes. Him. Aren't you still together, more or less?"

"No. He was smart, rather wonderful in a lot of ways. Not much of a lover, though, to tell you the truth. I don't mean just sex. Though that, too."

In the middle of the night he murmured to her, "You are indeed a force to be reckoned with."

He was glad to awaken first the next morning. He found his clothes and dressed in the living room, where a light still burned. In the kitchen he found a scratch pad, and turned past the grocery list ("cheese water lett grapes") and wrote a note. *You may have it. I'd like the dedication, though. No further demands.* He propped the pad against the coffee maker and left.

It had rained in the night, and dark, wet, slippery-looking leaves were plastered to the sidewalk. He walked the block to his car and wiped the moisture off the windows. In the next yard, a rotting jack-o-lantern was sinking like a melting snowman. The damp, gray day seemed fresh and new; he could have imagined he was in a new town. Interesting things were underway. He'd let the line go—what the hell!

He could probably use it anyway, and if anyone quibbled, he'd refer them to her. Maybe there should be something like a bank of lines, lines for borrowing. He wanted to say this to someone, and laugh.

His apartment-sharer, a fiction-writing student, said the next afternoon, "Out pretty late, weren't you. Big night, huh."

"Big enough." They were reasonably frank with one another, and it was a temptation to say more; it was an experience made for circulating. *Guess where I spent the night last night.*

It would trump dating a well-known novelist's daughter; it would trump almost any other kind of literary gossip.

But if it was the beginning of something, that something would require discretion. The following week, he hurried to the phone each time it rang, though each time he told himself it wouldn't be her, and it never was. In class, she showed no sign that anything was different, and neither did he. He was pleased with his circumspection: she'd trusted him not to blab, and he wouldn't. The pride he took in this sustained his restraint.

About the line, though—wasn't he free to tell? He let it slip here and there, and saw that his classmates looked at him with more respect than before.

But if, after that, they heard about the one-night stand, wouldn't they take it to be a simple transaction?

He resisted this thought. He was quite sure it wasn't a trade-off. There had come a happy moment when their instincts and sympathies meshed— (What sympathies? A little while earlier they'd been arguing. Oh—larger sympathies, about poetry. Etc.) Perhaps she wanted something more to come of it, too, but later, in the full light of day, saw the folly of going ahead with it. (He wasn't greatly practiced as a lover, but in the night she'd seemed to think he was more than satisfactory.) He thought about this a good deal.

Then the term was over. After the last class, people hung around saying goodbye; she was teaching only the one semester. He told her goodbye; she gave him a warm smile, took his hand for a moment, and thanked him for his good wishes. He couldn't help feeling that more would somehow come of this.

Her replacement next term was a man of moderate reputation, graying and a little deaf, author of many books of poetry that Sean thought rather dull. He was enthusiastic about almost all the student work. ("His praise is a *debased coinage*, if you ask me," Justine muttered.) He told Sean he saw a real advance in his work that term, and urged him to read various poets he'd already read.

At the last conference, he said to Sean, "Teaching's a funny business. You can be so wrong. I've seen people I thought had very modest talents make it pretty big. It's partly just sticking with it, working like a dog. Maybe you don't know whose talent *is* modest till later on." It sounded wise; but had the guy been trying to send him a message?

A copy of Bettina Thayer's latest book came, not from her with an inscription, but from the publisher, with a card that said "Compliments of the author." He found the poem dedicated to himself; his name on the page gave him a little *frisson* of feeling. A pretty good poem, his line neatly fitted in. If it was any longer his line.

When anyone asked later why he'd left the program and enrolled in law school, he would say, "Oh, it was all so competitive. Maybe I'll keep it up on my own."

Years later, he and his wife sometimes went on talking jags, often when they were lying in bed, and one evening he told her about his night with Bettina Thayer.

"You never told me that before! That's crazy, that she'd want a line, *one* line, that much! And a bit arrogant of her to think a one-night stand would get her whatever she wanted."

"Oh, it wasn't exactly that. It was just one of those moments . . . and it was a rather good line—you might look it up some time. Next to last line in her poem 'Ending.'" He admired his wife's intelligence and wit, but doubted that she'd read many poems since college—perhaps a few of the shortest scattered through popular magazines, if an unusual title or first line caught her eye. She'd look up his line, say it was good and she liked it, then forget it in a week.

"Oh, I don't doubt it, but it's still incredible. Was that the start of something, then?" The bedside lamps were still on, her magazine still open across her stomach; she stared at him appraisingly. "No? Well, she probably lost her nerve. Remembered the campus code or whatever."

"Maybe. I used not to think it was a trade, but maybe it was—sort of."

"And was she good in bed?"

"Indeed, yes."

"It's incredible, though, I can't believe it, wanting one line so much!"

Later, the light out, his wife lying snuggled against him, he pictured Bettina Thayer sitting close to him on the sofa in her cramped little living room, her warm hand in his, saying, "I love it as much as if I'd written it myself!"

The next-to-last line you said you wanted— A plain, even prosy poem. *That line of mine you took, what does it matter?* No. *That line of mine you lusted for one night*— Possibly. A plain piece, but nostalgic.

He might work on it. When he had the time. Which (it was almost a relief to know) wouldn't be any time soon.

THE OFFER

He was one of their best friends, and he was ill. He'd been ill for some time; now he seemed to be worse. "I ran into him downtown—he's not looking too good," the wife said to the husband. "Maybe we ought to invite him to dinner. I'll find out what he's allowed to eat."

They were eating on the screened porch, looking out at the river view. Sitting there over supper, the husband felt lucky: his pretty wife, with her yellow hair pulled up high at the back of her head; the good food they'd prepared together; their house here on the river, where a boat was passing, its wake splaying out behind it in thick, silvery waves. Speaking of their friend reminded him of the additional luck of good health.

Their friend didn't have either his health or a wife. He'd run through two wives already. "They wised up," he said cheerfully, and probably losing them had been his fault: in his healthier days he'd been known as a skirt-chaser. Now, three nights a week, he hooked himself up to a kidney machine.

"They're coming around to the idea of a transplant," the wife added. "When they can supply one. He looks sort of puffy. Puffy and resigned. He used to be so good-looking—well, he still is," she added loyally.

The friend came to dinner. He sat on the screened porch, and said how fine everything was. He was a little paunchy now and his face was going a bit jowly, but, as the wife had said, he was still good-looking, and his chinos were sharply creased, his loafers well polished.

The other guest was a woman they'd all known for years, and something about the occasion—the sick friend and his illness?—put her in a nostalgic mood. "That party you gave when you were living on Walker Street, remember that?" she said to him. (Maybe she believed this talk would be good for him.) "The night Dori Vincent's necklace broke and the beads ran down the hot air registers! She pretended they were valuable—maybe they were. That wonderful punch. . . ."

The husband began to feel impatient with these memories. Good times, yes, but a lot of those people were gone, some moved away, a few dead, a number of them divorced. He hadn't been married to his wife much of that time, and she might feel left out. But the sick man seemed to enjoy the reminiscences, and if there was something unconsciously elegiac in the train of thought, he seemed unaware of it. Still, the husband was glad to interrupt to point out the red kayak that came down the river, almost every night. They watched the paddle turning in the kayaker's hands, quick and rhythmical as a machine. They watched as the boat was overturned and then righted. Dark came to the woods across the river, and the last light shone in patches on the surface of the water.

After the guests were gone, the wife washed the good glassware, and the husband dried it. It was there at the sink, barefoot, still wearing her necklace, her dress swathed in a big apron, that the wife said dreamily, "You know—I think I'll donate a kidney for him."

What, are you crazy? he almost said. He waited a moment; he put some glasses on the shelf. Probably the wine and the evening's talk had brought on this great surge of feeling for their friend.

"Isn't it usually a relative? Anyway, we're talking major surgery here."

"Don't be silly. Anyone can donate. They ask when you get a driver's license."

"Wouldn't your organs be a tad old for this purpose?"

That was a mistake. "My dear! I am thirty-six years old and in excellent health."

"Of course you are. You're my healthy, beautiful wife. But I don't like to think of you taking that kind of risk. Listen. Let's leave the rest of this stuff. I can do it in the morning."

Upstairs, he undid the fastening of her necklace for her. He was thinking they ought to make love that night; it seemed important, almost essential. She agreed, without the enthusiasm he'd hoped for.

He almost brought up that crazy idea of hers in the next few days, to argue her out of it—but maybe she'd already forgotten it. A generous thought, of course, if totally far-fetched, and she *was* generous. She rarely looked to see what the contribution can at grocery checkout said before she pushed a dollar through the slot, and if everyone at the farmer's market had corn, she bought hers from the most downtrodden-looking seller. Her new idea, though, was beyond generosity and beyond most friendships. He taught in the same department at the college as the sick friend and had known him for years, far longer than she had, but it would never have occurred to him.

It was a miraculous procedure, of course. He was profoundly glad it had been perfected, or almost perfected; he hoped they could do it for him if he ever needed it. But surely the donor should be anonymous, if it wasn't your twin sister. This situation was not like anything he'd ever heard of.

The friend stayed on his mind. Once he'd come back after a sabbatical and found that a new textbook had been adopted in his absence. He'd stormed in to see the friend, who'd been acting head of the department that year; he'd announced in detail all that was wrong with the book, throwing in some witty and malicious criticism of the two colleagues who were just the sort to have chosen it. His friend listened politely; he had a large, innocent face under light, thinning, fly-away hair. He proved to be the one who'd pushed the committee into choosing the book; and he'd been willing to let the husband make a fool of himself over it. "Why the hell didn't you tell me right off!" the husband cried, laughing. "Oh, I thought it would be good for you to let it out," the friend said, slightly smug. Even the other night he'd had something like an air of complacency, aware that they were all thinking of him and his health. Or as if he knew important things they didn't know yet, things beyond the consultations with doctors and the working of his machine.

Good Lord, what was he doing, thinking such thoughts? This was a close friend, someone who felt close enough to him to confide his troubles, to report in confidence with his former wife's false accusations and imaginary wrongs. ("Mea culpa, but not *that* culpa.") This was the guy who read his articles and gave him careful, knowledgeable criticism before he sent them out to scholarly journals; the guy who'd called them in Rome the moment he heard they'd been robbed. Kind to his wife, accepting in a way not all of his friends had been. Some of them, particularly the women, seemed displeased that he'd married someone young and beautiful—younger and more beautiful than the woman he'd been living with when he met his wife. He'd lived with Jane for six years, and his friends acted as if they'd been married. She was a plumber, a plumber with a liberal arts degree, and he had admired the audacity of her choice of occupation, and the way she sat astride the lid of an ailing toilet, her back to the room, as if mounted on a horse and master of the situation. She'd been active in local politics, faxing letters to the papers and going to meetings in her pickup, sometimes accompanied by her black Lab. He'd had no idea how much his friends had approved of her till they split up.

Probably some of them wished to believe, because his wife was beautiful, that she was a bubblehead. Well, she was no bubblehead, but she was no academic and didn't need to be. He'd introduced her to some of his favorite books, and she'd loved them. She talked about them a little too enthusiastically; if, at parties, he heard her mentioning Kafka to the wrong person, he would go over and ease into the conversation to keep her from saying the obvious and exposing herself to the shrewd glances of those competitive faculty people.

"Why don't we know any other kind of people?" he said once, driving home after a party. He said it partly to sound her out. "I'm bored with these academics."

"I think they're wonderful, knowledgeable people! I'm crazy about some of them."

She might be crazy about them, but they'd have patronized her in a moment. The sick friend, healthier then, had not been one of them. When she talked to him, he listened and murmured, "Exactly." He told her about his research in mediaeval Italian history.

੬

The sick friend wanted to sell some things from his mother's estate that had been stored; the wife, who worked part-time at an antique shop, went over with her employer to look at his goods and make an offer.

That afternoon she came home bringing a small enameled box which contained a pair of earrings.

"He was so sweet. He said, 'You thought I'd forgotten about your birthday, didn't you.' He knows it's not anywhere near my birthday!" She stood at the mirror over the hall table, and put on the earrings. "Moonstones. They were his mother's. I was so touched."

"Lovely." He went closer to look at them. "I've never seen moonstones before." They were milky ovals set with a thin edge of gold. "Very becoming." He kissed her cheek.

"I didn't bring up the transplant business. I didn't want to get into it with Lucy there."

Why had he ever thought she'd forget it? All he wanted to say came avalanching into his mind. He watched her take the earrings off and put them back into the box. He'd better wait, though; he'd better say it exactly right.

They started supper preparations and he listened as she talked about her day.

"The old man who collects the Flow Blue china checked by. Just to say hello. No jokes today." This man told her what she called little risky jokes. "He wanted to talk, though. I told Lucy I was going to invite him to lunch some day, and she said, 'He'll keel over, he'll be so thrilled,' and I said, 'I don't promise to do mouth-to-mouth to bring him around.' But he's lonely."

They ate on the porch, and watched what passed on the river. A squarish pleasure boat with a striped canopy went slowly by; five or six people were on board, some sitting in chairs, one or two moving around. Closer, on the street down the hill below the house, the after-work traffic had diminished; occasionally a car had its lights on.

As they had coffee and biscotti, he got down to it. "About offering him a kidney." Surely she could hear in these very words the strangeness of it. "It *will* make him uncomfortable. It'll seem pretty *damned* odd, for one thing." He hadn't expected damned to pop out.

"It certainly won't! He'll be touched. He may try to talk me out of it—"

"Which is more than I can do," he said sourly. Some husbands would say, harshly: Forget it. Forget it right now! He wasn't that kind.

She swished her biscotto in the coffee and bit into it, frowning. In a moment she got up and silently took her cup into the kitchen. She was angry. He sat on, barely registering the kayaker who was moving along on the river.

What if the friend accepted, and there was a feature story in the paper? Oh, that was the least of it!

If he could analyze this—it was partly the thrilling thought of heroic self-sacrifice that had moved her. But beyond that?

There'd been a time seven years ago that he hadn't thought of in a long time until the last few days: a summer when she'd seemed keyed up and newly happy. Except that she was working more, nothing had changed; no new exercise program, no magic supplement from the health food store; regular summer weather, including a hot spell everyone else complained of and she seemed scarcely to notice. She was putting in more time with the antiques business, going with her employer to house sales and auctions, sometimes out of town; in the past she had done this occasionally, and complained about the time it took. Now she went on complaining. "Lucy wants me to be as wrapped up in it as she is. She's so disappointed if I don't want to go!" She complained over and over, and was giddy with happiness.

"Listen, let me go to the auction with you," he said one Saturday afternoon. "Where is it?" He'd surprised himself: he hadn't thought this out before he spoke.

She made a strange little sound, surely involuntary. Perhaps it was "Oh" in some level beyond his hearing. She paled; he half-expected her to say, "I feel dizzy, I'd better sit down," or, "I have the most appalling headache all of a sudden." She stared at him. "Oh! I think—I don't know if Lucy would like the idea, it's all business with her—"

He was terrified. He'd almost picked up something ready to explode. She was still staring at him. He had a sense of things in motion as if the house might be quivering slightly.

"Oh, it's O.K., it was just a passing thought," he said. She kissed him goodbye and left, and he sat down in the living room, exhausted.

For a week or two afterwards, he'd worked on perfecting the right remark. "You seem as happy as a woman who's found a new lover." No, a crude joke, a crude sounding-out. How about, "You seem so happy these days"? But if, after a moment, she said, "Yes. I haven't wanted to tell you, but. . . ."? Some days he knew they would be divorced, and he thought of Jane; he saw her smiling sardonically. "All that excess charm!" she'd said after they met the future wife at a party. "I wonder if she was ever Miss Teenage Something-or-Other, there's a bit of that about her," not scornful, but gently superior—and Jane stayed in his mind, her serious face, innocent of makeup, her feet in their stout work boots, her spicy tofu and earnest talk. She'd seemed, as he prepared to move, an especially fine person, almost a sister, and he'd wanted to stay friends with her, and she'd say yes, of course, then added, "Molly"—the Lab—"will certainly miss you." Now when he saw her in the co-op or at some university lecture, she gave him only a slight smile, if she looked at him at all. He wondered if she ever drove past the house and saw on the stoop the ceramic dog that his wife dressed in a sou'wester and a child-sized yellow slicker when it rained, a watch cap in winter, and a yachting cap in summer. Yes, he told Jane mentally, it's a bit cute, but why not? I love her and she's my wife—though I don't know for how much longer.

He waited. It's O.K., he told himself; nothing much has changed, really. In the mirror he looked older and more boring, his short, furry brown hair hopelessly old-fashioned, his nose thin and pinched; there was a baffled, almost hopeless look in his eyes. He studied the haircuts of younger men, but decided against them. He bought a new summer jacket, and she said she liked it.

Then, suddenly, her good spirits were gone. She was quiet and unsmiling. When he muttered one evening, "What happened to the good corkscrew?—it's supposed to be in this drawer," she turned from making the salad and cried fiercely, "How the hell would I know!" then burst into tears.

"Oh. I'm sorry," he said, but neutrally; he touched her shoulder. He sensed that the crisis was past, and felt out of patience for the first time.

Things began to tilt toward the normal. One night, when they spoke of love, she said, "You're good to me, I don't really deserve you."

"Of course not, who could deserve me?" he said lightly, thinking, *no more. I don't need to know any more.*

He should have let her tell him; he'd have forgiven her. If there'd been anything, that is. Now he had to find out. He could ask her about it tonight. He could begin by asking if she could remember how their friend's illness had progressed, and exactly what shape he was in seven years ago.

But he held off till bedtime. In the bedroom, she said matter-of-factly, as if there were no quarrel between them, "About him. I have to put it to him the right way, so he knows I'm serious, not just making a gesture. He's got to understand that he can really take me up on it." She was pulling off her camisole, a soft cream color she'd told him was called "candlelight." "Or that he can say no, and I won't feel put down or keep on talking about it—you know. You understand."

"Yes. Yes," he said, and they got into bed and soon plunged into lovemaking, as if they were in perfect accord.

Driving home from school now, he sometimes detoured by the friend's house on afternoons when the wife wasn't working. They wouldn't be making love, the friend wouldn't be up to it, but there must be the old residue of feeling. Thinking of them sitting together, kissing lightly, holding hands, gave him a feeling of odd, free-floating lust. But her car, the Dadmobile, the Buick her father had given her when he got a new one, was never there when he went by, and of course it was ridiculous to have looked.

"Have you called him lately?" she would ask; and he would call. Sometimes the friend reported that he'd received a letter from an old acquaintance, someone he hadn't heard from in years who had somehow learned of his illness; they would talk about this old acquaintance and what he was doing now. The husband was touched and troubled by the thought that the people who wrote might be saying goodbye. Surely things weren't at that pass: the sick friend said he was on a waiting list for a transplant, and that his prospects were said to be good. The husband arranged to drop by with some videos he and his wife had enjoyed. Driving home, he would think: nothing happened. Nothing at all.

The wife's sister came for a visit, and talked the wife into driving with her up to the Mall of the Americas. She was gone; he was alone. Alone to think about it; to think what to ask and how to ask it, which ought to be easier with her out of the house. But he knew already that she'd bat his questions away; she knew he couldn't ask their friend. She'd laugh them off, the way she'd laughed it off when she'd lost the gas tank cap to his car, treating it as if it had been a charming little prank. And how stupid for her to be gone now, up to that giant mall!

Too bad he couldn't hook himself up to a machine like the friend, and get this poison out of his system. Consult a counselor? A friend? (The sick friend was the only one he'd ever been close enough to for that.) Through the skylight over the bed he saw, one morning, two softly dissolving jet streams crossed in a giant X—did that mean something?

The wife came back with a lavender check shirt for him, and a bad cold that turned into bronchitis and laryngitis. The husband took breakfast upstairs to her a couple of mornings, urged her to rest, and brought her books to read. In the past, whenever she was reading something he'd recommended, he liked to pick up the book when she wasn't actually reading it and re-read a little of it himself, not so much to talk about it as to experience again what she was experiencing, to be inside her mind for a time; it gave him pleasure. He didn't feel like doing that now, and brought her only the latest mysteries.

Her voice began to return. One morning she said softly, "Don't forget to call him," meaning the sick friend. "Ask how he is, tell him I'm sick but thinking about him."

The sick friend was apparently sicker than anyone had realized. When another friend phoned with the bad news, the husband was astounded; he was as surprised as if his friend had never been sick a day in his life.

He was at home that afternoon, and he decided to call his wife at work, partly to alleviate the lonely feeling the news had given him. "Oh, my God," she muttered when he told her. "Well. I'll see you a little later." He expected her to have more to say than that; but of course she was at work. He'd thought she might even come home, though that didn't make sense.

As they got dressed for the memorial service a week later, she said, "I offered. I told him I would. He just laughed. I said, 'I'm serious'—it was when I stopped by one day. But he said no, there'd be one available pretty soon. But you know, maybe it was too late for anything like that, that's what I'm wondering." She had put on a dark suit and looked very fine; she was putting on the moonstone earrings.

"It was generous of you," he muttered. She hadn't mentioned this before, but perhaps that had been in deference to his doubts. That she mentioned it now, when she didn't have to, ought to be proof that there were no old guilts behind it.

He wasn't thinking about the friend any more than he could help; it was too frightening. As a small child he'd visited a grandmother who'd been obsessively worried about a couple of abandoned wells on her farm; the wells had been filled with brush and dirt, but the grandmother warned him to be careful where he stepped; if the ground gave under him, he must move in a hurry. Now he tried not to step out onto the shaky ground of his loss.

During the service, he observed the people who sat around them in the church and tried to occupy his thoughts with them, and with an article he'd been working on. When it was time for a hymn, there was a rustling as people rose and turned to the right place. He and his wife shared a hymn book, and as they sang he told himself he was glad she had made the offer. It had been true, if naïve, friendship. He was glad, very glad. The hymn ended, and they sat down once more.

It was necessary to have trust. What was marriage without trust? He closed his eyes as determinedly as if he would never open them again. Nothing had happened. What if it had? What if people knew? (And smiled because he didn't?) No one knew, and anyway, his friend was dead, very dead. Which he would certainly never consider a relief. Never.

The minister was beginning to pray; he bowed his head, a little late, and prayed too. He prayed that he and his wife would again sit out on the screened porch of an evening; they would watch the kayak pass, turn over, and right itself again. Sitting there, he would again be able to mourn his friend, and think of him with simple sorrow and affection. It would happen; it would happen.

THE SKY FADING UPWARD TO YELLOW: A FOOTNOTE TO LITERARY HISTORY

You know what happens after someone like Worsham dies. In no time, hardly longer than it takes to say "important literary figure" or "publishing house," the wheels begin to turn. Maybe the first wife starts work on a memoir of the early years; the second or third wife gets busy preparing some letters or papers for publication. Eventually a letter soliciting information for a biography appears in *The New York Times Book Review* and *The New York Review of Books*. However it goes, the wives tend to get their due, their day in court—the wives and the long-term alliances.

Brenda was a short-term alliance, but she felt she deserved a page in Worsham's life story. She thought about this a good deal. Whenever I was back in town on a visit, we talked about it. She was still there where we'd gone to graduate school—where we'd gone expecting, like so many others, to become writers, and where, one year, Robert Worsham was our teacher. It was customary there to bring big names out for a semester or a year, and he was a big name. He was in his fifties then, but hadn't been in the teaching business long; at that point in his career he could pick and choose, a semester here, a summer conference there. He died three or four years later, suddenly, and before long a volume of his letters was in the works, "awfully soon," Brenda said, authoritatively. She had a bunch of letters from him herself, but was not surprised that nobody asked about them. "Madeleine's in charge, and she may not know even now that I exist." (Madeleine was his wife.) But when Brenda learned that a man named Dozier was at work on a biography, she began to expect a letter, a kind of summons. "He's been in touch with people who knew about us." She was resigned, ready to be reasonable about it. "I could refuse to tell him anything, but sometimes if you don't cooperate, people will try to piece it together anyway and get it all wrong. *He* used to tell a story about that."

"Anybody who's writing about him ought to be in touch with Bren," Jed, her friend, said. "She's the one who was closest to him that year. She knows things nobody else would know. What he was thinking about—his inner life." He looked at her fondly across our booth at Whaley's, a tavern that had once been the writers' hangout. Jed and I were on one side, Brenda on the other, her back against the wall, her legs out full-length on the seat. It was afternoon, but inside the light was dim. Out on the bright street there was some spring street work going on, with intermittent jackhammering, students jaywalking around the work, townspeople going up and down the sidewalk. Brenda often spoke in an affectedly soft voice, and she waited for a lull in the noise to murmur, "There was a week—when I was quite sure he was going to crack up. I was planning what to do, who to call." She shook her head, shrugged, and reached for a cigarette, her hand trembling for an instant, and I wondered what old excitement, what old regret for the past she was feeling.

Jed seemed so interested in the Brenda-Worsham connection that I wondered if knowing about it had helped attract him to her. I could imagine him writing a friend, "You'll like her—a remarkable woman, gifted and vital, once mistress of a famous novelist." He was a sculptor, a curly-haired, solidly built man, his body type not unlike Worsham's. He smiled at her encouragingly and said, "You have to put personal interests aside, in this kind of thing. If he gets in touch, you'll have to level with him and show him the letters."

"Oh, you'll hear from him, surely," I said. I really thought she would.

ễ

But she didn't. The subject came up again the next time I was through town. My folks were still living in Illinois then, and I got back to the Midwest at least a couple of times a year.

"He has to have been in touch with Andrea and Herb," she said. They were the ones from our bunch of Worsham students who had achieved some reputation; Andrea had published an interview with him, among other things. They knew about Brenda for sure, but Andrea hadn't liked her. Anyway, Andrea and the others might have considered it a breach of taste or judgement to bring up the Brenda connection now. (There was Mrs. W. off in the East.) Brenda seemed to be having the same thought. "I begged him, I implored him to tell her, get the pain over now, it will be better for us all in the long run! I remember one night they talked on the phone half an hour, and when he came back into the room he said, 'How we batter and bruise each other with *words*,' and I really thought he might break down and cry. They'd had trouble before—they'd always had trouble. He said once, 'Madeleine makes it sound as if my success is a species of morbid condition, brought on by a doting mother and doubting father. She once said I must have been "cruelly programmed to strive for success."' Brenda pressed her lips together, as if to keep from saying too much.

I'd just been reading the Worsham letters and hadn't found much in them about their troubles, but of course his wife had made the selection. "Too bad the timing wasn't better for you two," I said, "too bad you couldn't have found him sitting next to you in class, another student—"

She was taking some peanuts from a bowl on the table— we were once again in Whaley's—and she held them right in her fist for a moment and looked at me suspiciously. "Oh, you think I was drawn to his success? I can tell you, name and fame were not in it. I'd have seen him for what he was anywhere. Reflected glory is *not* my thing."

"No, no, I didn't mean that," and I didn't—at least I don't think I did. "No, I just meant, what rotten luck, Brenda."

"B.—an aloof exhibitionist." That's what I wrote in my journal before I began to like her. (We were big on journals and descriptions back then.) There was some truth in it: she wanted our attention, then seemed to throw it away. She was small, lithe, bright-eyed, with high-colored cheeks, as if she'd just scrubbed them almost too hard. She was from the East and had been to Europe, and had little anecdotes of Roman pensions and channel ferries; I remember her saying of someone, some obscure writer she'd met abroad, that he spoke French "in a soft, Belgian sort of way." I was at heart a Midwesterner, sensitive about expressions with "corn" in them, such as "corn-fed," and hungry for a personal style; Brenda made me feel large and innocent, and I took her in carefully. After a while we hit it off together, and when the woman who was sharing her apartment left town, she spoke of my moving in. Then she said the roommate might be back. That never happened, but other possibilities were developing.

One night late in the fall a bunch of us, six or seven, had dinner at her place. Worsham was the guest of honor. Everybody brought something, and we ate off our laps and the coffee table, and took in what he had to say. He was a short, compact man, his head somehow especially compact-looking, as if it had a high specific gravity—solid as a rock; he had smoker's teeth and a slightly weathered face, but looked remarkably young all the same. I thought it was exactly the way he ought to look, and when I saw, later, a picture of him handsome in his twenties, I felt that the way we had known him was his true appearance, the way he was meant to be.

We questioned him steadily. We wanted to know what to think about everything, especially all the other writers in the world. Who was Good? Who was worth our important while? He didn't serve up the little insider's anecdotes we might have hoped to hear, though once in a while a question would make him laugh a short, sincere, cheerful laugh. "Him? Sure, he's good. It's too bad his life has turned progressively less interesting, since it's all he's got to write about." I remember he said something about reading a little Hemingway from time to time "to cleanse the palate. Like the sherbet between the courses? Not too much at a time, though." Someone asked about the novel he was working on, and he talked about his grandfather, who figured in it. The grandfather had taken Robert Worsham and his brother on a trip to Canada when they were nine and eleven. The grandfather had taken sick, and Robert had had to walk miles into the nearest town for help. It was early morning; he remembered the mist hanging over a stream, and the day beginning to warm up, and the thrilling and frightening feeling of being set free into adulthood. He was so much, he understood so much about himself and the rest of the world and described it so well it made you long to see more—to go out and see and understand.

Some of the rival talk that night had stayed in my mind. It was a time of overalls and granny dresses, and Brenda had on a long flowered dress and brown lace-up boots that Worsham said resembled high-top shoes from the turn of the century. "When I see my daughter in overalls," he said, "I think of it as homage to the American farmer." Someone remarked that homage to the past was in style—those secondhand store dresses of the forties and fifties. And the Goodwill-look: homage to the downtrodden. "What's Brenda's dress homage to?" someone asked.

We waited for Worsham to answer; he was nice about paying attention to all the silly things we said. "Oh, all the old-fashioned women, I suppose. A paradox in itself—" glancing at her quickly. A mysterious look passed between them; I was wild to know what it meant. But he only got up and opened another bottle of wine. He seemed to know where everything was in the kitchen without having to ask.

He was still there when the rest of us went home. His coat was on a chair by the door, yet he seemed somehow settled in. It was late—we'd been waiting for him to leave—and it was cold, and LaDeane Hilderbrand and I set off together, walking fast, moaning over the cold, our caps down over our ears, our scarves up over our chins. We trotted along rapidly not only from the cold, but because we were in a hurry to get far enough away to start talking. "Have they got something going, or are they just about to?" she puffed.

"God! he's only been here two months!" ("God!" was something Brenda said a good deal.) "How do you suppose it happens! Wouldn't you like to know which one—but I thought he had a family back East. Well, some women are determined to find someone older, a married man. *Father* was a married man—"

"Oh, come on, she just wanted to make him comfortable, give him a home away from home," LaDeane said, and we burst into crazy laughter. "Of course, this is only jealousy, you know that," meaning it couldn't be. We were shivering from excitement as much from the cold; probably we both had trouble going to sleep that night.

I don't remember any more catty talk about Brenda and Worsham after that night. It would be hard to say, considering their great discretion, how all of us knew what was going on, but we were people who went in for observation. And soon we all felt too loyal to pass judgment. In some odd way, the affair with Brenda might have seemed to make him more one of us. We felt we were his friends and family, and he told us things that I doubt we'd have heard if he had been living safely at home. One night at a party, when Brenda happened to be home with a cold, he and I talked a long time. I asked what he would be doing the next year, and he said, "I've got some hard choices to make." Choices involving Brenda?—I preferred to believe the question was larger. "When I was your age, I expected to achieve complete wisdom by the age of forty," with a resigned little smile. "But these decisions are no easier than they ever were."

I was eager to tell him he must do what would make him happiest. He laughed. "That's the hard part. Happiest now or later? You'll never be in this predicament, of course, you're too level-headed and sensible."

"Oh, no, not at all! I'm not sensible at all!" I cried hopefully.

"It'll save you time, days and weeks of your life. That's what I have to think about right now. *Time.* There's only so much of it."

I didn't tell anyone else, including Brenda, what he'd said, but hoarded it as though it were important. And if the rest of us didn't discuss Brenda and Worsham or know quite how to look at it, it wasn't from lack of thinking about it. I dreamed about Brenda's apartment; once, inside it in a dream, I told Worsham that Brenda had left town, like the roommate I'd been going to replace. He said it was all right.

Brenda and I went East together over spring break that year. Over vacation Worsham went back to New York, to domestic arrangements unknown to me and perhaps to Brenda as well. This time she was going East too. She'd bought an old car, a sedan of a dull, lusterless brown, the color of dried mud, with an inefficient muffler that made it sound like a motorboat, Worsham said. "We're coming in to the dock!" he cried once as we stopped in front of his place, giving him a ride home from at the after-class gathering at Whaley's.

We drove East in the brown car, dropping Herb Soles in Athens, Ohio, then Brenda, proposed that we veer down into West Virginia to see a friend of hers. We didn't know much about driving in the mountains, and the last twenty or thirty miles we had no brakes to speak of. The friend she was looking for wasn't around, but we got the brakes worked on, and while we waited we walked around town, and sat down in a little café near the garage. I could see Brenda taking it all in. The beer truck driver came in, trundling his cases along. As he was leaving, the woman at the cash register, thirtyish and pretty, with a wretched permanent, gave him a hopeful smile and said, "Leaving us so soon?" and he thought for a moment and said, "Better come with me." "Observe, Rachel, that's how it's done in the real world," Brenda said. "You notice how much prettier she was when she was talking to him?" "A man and a maid, no music necessary," I said, an allusion to "Guy de Maupassant," an Isaac Babel story I'd been reading in the car. And I thought that the man and women there had it easy, their thoughts and motives being so much simpler than Brenda's and Worsham's. About that I may have been wrong.

We went on to Nyack, where her mother lived, and next morning there was the Hudson down at the foot of the lawn, in the beautiful morning mist. Her mother looked at us dubiously, even after we got cleaned up, Brenda barefoot, wearing her faded Dostoevsky tee-shirt, me in the department store pants and pullover outfit that I already knew wasn't quite right.

Brenda took me into the city and showed me the sights very pleasantly, as if I were some visiting aunt. I had assumed that going East included seeing Worsham, and I half-expected to see him step out from some shadowy corner at the Cloisters, from the lunch line at the museum, or in the Japanese restaurant where we had dinner. Perhaps I was even disappointed. Keyed up from being there and from trying to take it all in coolly, I said something gauche about wondering if he was in town.

Brenda smiled tolerantly. "Have I heard from him? No, I have not. He's free, and I'm free, we don't control each other. I told him I might be going home, but I didn't give him my phone number because it would have been a direction. He can take extraordinary measures if he wants to get in touch, but there's no obligation. We're free, both of us. No strings attached."

"That's wonderful," I said. "That's the way it ought to be. Free, absolutely free."

There were a couple of months left in the term when we got back. We had a great party near the end, afternoon to evening to morning, finally tossing the glasses out into the yard, a ceremony the meaning of which I have forgotten, and I suppose all it meant to the neighbors was drunk-and-disorderly. That afternoon we'd sat around in the sun, Worsham sitting there smiling—a cheerful drinker, someone called him, and he said, "The Lord loveth a cheerful drinker." Once he nodded off for a few minutes. People were still asking him questions now and again: last chance for instructions before we parted company. I think we felt almost apprehensive about his going away and leaving us.

Portions of the Worsham biography appeared in a couple of quarterlies after two or three years. One of them had a short passage about the year he'd taught us. As I read it, I thought how fine that year had been, even finer than we'd known at the time. It made me feel both happy and sad.

Brenda was reading it too. She called me a few days later. "So much missing!" She meant herself and their 'relationship'.

"In the end I couldn't stand it," she said. "I started writing what I know about that year, I really couldn't help it. Well, actually I'd already written a little of it down. I'm amazed at how much there is! But now I don't know whether to send it to Dozier or not, this and the letters I have. The book hasn't been announced for next year so he probably hasn't finished it. Should I send it?"

"I don't know. I hadn't thought about it."

"I was keeping a journal, and I wrote down what we talked about, what was on his mind. It was seven months, more or less, one of the last good writing years of his life. He was finishing the last book and planning the one he didn't get to finish. A pretty important time."

Her tone suggested she meant not only to set me straight, but now, years later, to set Worsham straight too. Oh, doesn't every woman, no matter how often she's said they're free, doesn't she, deep down, expect the man freely to give up all others for her? I thought of them sitting side by side in a booth in Whaley's, smiling with an unanimity of gaze and an air of great happiness, as if they'd just had some wonderful news. Wasn't it enough? It wasn't, thank God, my job to sort out what this meant in their lives in the long run, but there it was, it had happened, with all its joy of discovery. But she wanted more: a page in his history; a paragraph, a footnote. She may have felt it was a kind of belated gift that he'd have wanted her to have.

"Sure, you know the inside story—the lowdown." I said it lightly, though I knew the tone might not please her. "But I don't know. Maybe you should let it sit for a while and see how it looks later."

She'd expected me to say send it on, send it on. She said stiffly, "I don't know what I'll decide. I haven't finished it yet anyway."

☙

I told Tim, my companion, about the call. He and I were living farther west, where I was working on a wildlife protection magazine and he worked with a public interest research group. He's a do-er, rather different from a lot of my old graduate school friends. He's read a fantastic amount, but he says it's a mistake to know the people who wrote the books: if the book's any good, what more do you need?

He'd just come in from clearing the snow from the driveway, and was in his sock feet, warming up by the stove. When I told him about my call from Brenda, he shrugged. "To blab or not to blab? Well, it was a lot like your everyday run-of-the-mill affair, wasn't it? Except that he was Somebody. Wanting to consummate the union with Success! There's something kind of primitive about it. As if the magic will rub off on you."

"It didn't seem so run-of-the-mill at the time. It seemed terribly exciting and important. And he was a really nice person. And she was drawn to the things that made him a success, not just his *being* one." I was sounding a little too intense. "Well, anyway, it's literary history, like Sheilah Graham and Scott Fitzgerald, or Hemingway and his loves. Or maybe it's not like anybody else at all, but it's still interesting to a lot of people."

"That poor guy deserves to have his old flings cloaked in a decent obscurity, as much as any suburbanite," Tim said. I couldn't tell whether he was serious or not; on certain subjects he likes to tease me.

❦

"I've finished it," Brenda said first thing the next time she called. Sometimes she'd begun by telling me the news—what she was working on at the university press, what Jed was working on (sometimes an important sculpture commission for some public lawn), or news about their daughter. This evening she got right down to business.

"What? Oh, the Worsham piece," I said—as if I didn't know. I think it was the moment when I first knew I was sick of her important recollections.

She read it to me; we must have been on the phone nearly an hour. She was proud of all there was to tell, all the things that would be useful to anyone writing about his work: a different ending he had considered for the book he was finishing, and the plot of the unfinished one—a version of his parents' lives, beginning with his mother, before her marriage, in a sanitarium at Saranac, where she had some sort of romance. ("Like in *The Magic Mountain*," I murmured, and Brenda said, "Well, not really.") Wouldn't this be in his papers?—maybe not all of it. Her journal recorded where they had been when he told her certain things—eating take-out food at her place, or riding through the thawing countryside in the spring after she got the car, which he called the Mud Hen.

"I talk about the first time we had dinner together and went to my place afterwards and talked. The next week I invited him to come with me to see *It Happened One Night* on the campus film series, and we had coffee afterwards. I say 'One night later that week there was a wonderful thick fog, and I called him and asked if he'd been outside, it was such a mysterious, magical night. He said he'd walk over to my place, it wasn't far, and we took a long walk together. We became lovers, and he often stayed over at my apartment.' Isn't that all right?"

She described an afternoon of sentiment when he'd given her a ring. A ring from a machine, the kind you see beside the bubble gum machine up at the front of supermarkets or variety stores: you put in a nickel and get a prize in a little plastic bubble, one of four or five kinds. They got some of the wrong ones before they got a ring, and Worsham tried to give the excess to a child standing nearby, but the child moved away in alarm. They continued their walk, through downtown and across campus to the river. On the footbridge they stopped, and he put the ring on her finger. It was December, and it was cold on the bridge, but a still, windless cold. They kissed and walked on, her hand in his pocket—she didn't want to put her glove back on over the ring. (I could picture it, a toy with adjustable prongs of the sort that break off if you adjust it too often, though that ensures you'll toss it out before it turns green.) They went on to the art building, and into the gallery; she remembered what he said about some of the pictures. When they went back over the bridge, it was past sunset, the sky flushed orange along the horizon and fading upward to yellow, the water reflecting the color; little greenish lights blossoming across the river.

The next year, after he was back East (reconciled with his wife? Brenda didn't say; she dealt more in moments than continuity), she put the ring in an envelope and wrote on it the time and place and his name. Now she had written an account of the important moments.

The sky fading upward to yellow! And what he said about the pictures in the museum. I'd been caught up in the account in spite of myself; it seemed almost part of my past too, since I'd been there with them in that important year, and he was my teacher and she my friend. But how much did what she was telling me matter? A great deal, in one sense, and much less in another. I thought, not then but later, of a line from that Auden poem about Yeats, changing it: He was foolish like us.

And while she was talking I pictured Worsham as he used to look walking along alone, maybe across the street from me, unaware of my notice. He had a tight, secretive walk, ambling along, hands in pockets, and I would imagine he was pondering lives known to him only, fictional people and events he was trying to understand and shape. That glimpse of him always gave me a moment of deep happiness. Now he was gone, the worlds in his head gone with him. I didn't like to think that people who hadn't read much of him or fully taken in what they read (hadn't loved it enough?) would one day be poking into the secret recesses of his life.

"Without this," Brenda said, "Any account of that year is so incomplete it's, well, kind of ridiculous, really."

"There's always a lot missing, expect maybe in Boswell. I don't know. Some of these biographies—it's just career stuff, it's just a job. Half the time they don't care for the subject that much, and they don't always get the essence."

"They won't if people don't tell them what happened. This man may not be Boswell, who *is*, but what he's done so far is O.K. But you don't think I should send it! If you had this stuff, would you just sit on it? Really? I don't believe you would." Her tone was knowing: was I jealous?

"I wouldn't tell anyone in the world. Anyone at all!" It gave me a mysterious thrill to say it, though this had never occurred to me before. "But you want to send your stuff, so— send it. You won't be happy till you do."

A silence fell; I'd given some slight offense. I'd meant to.

But we were old friends, and I'd always given her a kind of precedence in our friendship; in a minute I was smoothing it over. "What a good teacher he was! Remember when your story about the house sitter was on that worksheet? That was a good story, Brenda. Maybe you should turn that year into fiction."

"Oh, it's occurred to me. Actually, I've started a novel—maybe more like a novella. I still might be a little close to it."

"You might make something really good out of it. There's an authenticity about what actually happened. That's what you ought to do!" Probably I persuaded myself that I was sincere.

I bought the Worsham biography as soon as it came out. When I got home from the bookstore it was lunchtime, and Tim was already eating, but before I ate I sat down and read the section about his year with us. There it was: where he lived, and what he said in his letters and notebook about his landlady, a Rosicrucian, and about the other faculty and his classes; what he was working on, what he was reading. There was more than in the magazine installment, and yet how bare-bones it seemed—empty of the old excitement. I put the book aside till later.

Brenda called. "It's pretty good," she said, sounding regretful, and I understood she was sorry not to have sent him her stuff.

"It's O.K. Not all that could be hoped for, but O.K."

"Will there ever be one good enough for you? For us?"

"Probably not. How's your novel coming?"

"Oh, I've put it aside for the moment. I don't know if it's going to work. . . . His last stories are coming out, you know, and I read in the *Times* that somebody's been selected to piece his unfinished novel together. There'll be another biography in a few years." Still time to offer her letters and memoir.

"Sure." What was the use of saying I'd never read another?

How ridiculous it was! That was what I thought that evening as I sat reading in the living room while Tim did some paperwork at the kitchen table. How ridiculous! The other people in our class knew what had happened between Brenda and Worsham; it was not a secret. I couldn't even say why I'd wanted her to keep quiet. Telling all had simply seemed to me—*unseemly.*

I'd started to reread Worsham, and it was one his books that was in my lap as I sat there. I was half-reading, half-thinking, and I wanted to murmur to Brenda, or even to the world at large: Here he is. This is all we need.

TOWARD THE END: VARIATIONS ON A THEME

I—THE SINGING

Each night, one of the girls in the family went down the hill to spend the night with the grandmother. From the family's backyard a path ran through an empty field, clear as the part in a head of hair; it led to the backyard of the grandmother's trim and modest house.

The daughter's family, which supplied the girls, lived in the old house up the hill. The house came with working the land, which the daughter's husband did; he'd fallen into this by marrying the daughter. He might not have intended to marry her to start with—hard to say about that. He'd married her, though, having got her in trouble; sometimes he seemed to look around in surprise, seeing himself the father of five. Her family was as decent as his, and less countrified; a number of her sisters had married men from "off" and gone to live in Charlotte. They came back on Sundays every so often, wearing more stylish clothes than their country sister did, and at holidays and family reunions they brought food and dodged around one another between the kerosene stove and the wood-burning range in the grandmother's kitchen; a smell of strong coffee would come from that end of the house. Outside, their husbands stood around the backyard, smoking cigars. That was what Cornelia, one of the daughters of the country family, remembered later: the smell of coffee and cigar smoke, and a vague sweet smell of cake. Later she thought of those times oftener than her sisters did, and thought oftener of her grandmother; probably that was because she'd been the one sleeping with her grandmother the night the mysterious thing happened.

The four girls of the country family admired their Charlotte relatives; they didn't seem to resent not having citified things. They didn't seem troubled by living in a house older than the grandmother's—their great-grandparents' house, long-weathered almost black, one of the windows still an ancient swing-out wooden closure. The girls were close together in age, and perhaps comradeship kept them happy. Younger, they had fought and cried and cheered up again; they seemed to know how to get over things. Their mother didn't spoil them: having not been strict enough with herself to keep from getting into trouble, she was strict about everything else now, especially when members of her family were visiting. "You get those dishes washed up now, and wipe off the stove—" She was given to trifling complaints, and kept one of them out of school to help her every washday.

They went along, not worrying much. They seemed to understand that their mother lived a life of baffled improvisation, struggling for respect she would probably never get. The girls concentrated on the good times, the visits from relatives down at the grandmother's house, and the Sunday afternoons in summer when a couple of boys might show up in a rattling, backfiring car that came to rest in the yard as if with its last breath. The girls would drag out some straight chairs from the kitchen or dining room and they would all sit out in the yard in the shade near the grape arbor.

And always, before twilight, the one whose turn it was went down the hill to the grandmother's house and at bedtime climbed into the high double bed beside her.

It was quieter at the grandmother's than at home, and easier to do homework, and Cornelia didn't mind when her week to sleep down the hill came around. She went down the steep path carrying some school books, dodging the cockleburs. She and her grandmother talked while Cornelia washed the dishes. Then she did her eighth-grade homework at the kitchen table. She was a short girl with dull yellow-brown hair, her nose and mouth pinched a bit close together for beauty.

She was tired; she'd helped pick beans at home before she came down the hill. She got into bed on the side nearest the wall (the grandmother would have to get up in the night), and she was ready to sleep; she and the grandmother exchanged a few words about the cover, and said goodnight. Her grandmother turned down the lamp, blew out the flame, and Cornelia fell deeply asleep.

She didn't know what time it was when she realized her grandmother was sitting up in bed, speaking. "Somebody's singing out there! Listen to that singing!"

Cornelia didn't want to wake up; she was deep in a dream and deeply happy there, and she couldn't let go of it. She hadn't heard anything from outside, and didn't want to. She made a vague sound and went on sleeping.

She came awake a little later with the feeling that some time had passed. Her grandmother was gone from the bed, and Cornelia knew, as if she had registered it in sleep, that her grandmother was outdoors. Painfully, she forced herself out of the grip of sleep, and slid out of bed.

It was a mild night in early September, and her grandmother, in her long-sleeved nightgown, stood in the middle of the graveled backyard.

"Did you see anybody, Ma?" That was what the girls called the grandmother—what their mother called her.

"No. No. I didn't see anybody. But I heard that singing."

I was afraid for her, Cornelia said later: I was afraid for her, out there in her nightgown, and I told her we better go back in the house. She said it because she realized she should have been afraid. But she hadn't been; it had seemed reasonable to be standing there in bright moonlight, listening. Maybe she'd heard a drift of far-off music herself; later she wondered.

They went back inside and latched the screen door.

"It was the prettiest singing," the grandmother said as they got back into bed.

The grandmother spoke of it later to her daughters, but in a matter-of-fact way, and they all told her she ought not to have gone out of the house, oh, no. Who knew who or what might have been out there! They asked the closest neighbor up the road if any of his boys had been out that night, passing on the road. He was somewhat hurt: his boys came in at a reasonable hour, and they would never do anything that might disturb Miss Myra.

❦

The grandmother died a few months later. She'd insisted on going to the Armistice Day parade in town: one of her sons had fought in the First World War, and though he hadn't been killed and had died only a few years before, she got on the school bus and rode into town to see the parade of school children that, in those mid-thirties' years, marched uptown from the school while the town band played patriotic songs. She stood watching, a small withered figure in a black coat and hat in the small crowd on the sidewalk. It was windy, and the day was colder than she'd expected, though knowing it would be this cold wouldn't have kept her away.

Somehow, she missed the school bus going home; maybe she tried to flag it down somewhere on the sidewalk and the driver didn't see her. Or maybe it was against the rules to take anyone except school children, and the neighbor boy who drove it had picked her up out in the country but was afraid to stop in town. She walked along, heading toward home, and knocked on the door of a house where she knew the family, people related by marriage to one of her daughters. The son of the family drove her home.

A week later she was ill, and the illness turned into pneumonia. It was her last illness. If only she hadn't stubbornly gone to that parade! her daughters said.

❦

After her grandmother died, the night she'd heard the singing lingered in Cornelia's mind. Maybe the music had been a portent, something otherworldly—she would have liked to believe that, but no one else had thought so, and her mother often made fun of superstitions. At the time, one of the aunts had said, "It was just some dream she had, that's what it was."

Cornelia thought of it later, living with her husband in another old house down in the next county, a slightly more backward section than the one where she had grown up. She was old; her children were grown. She had more time to think now, and she thought of that night. Probably by now almost no one else remembered it.

She understood perfectly why her grandmother would get out of bed to find the mysterious music. The prettiest singing! her grandmother said. The moonlight had silvered everything, making deep shadows beneath the old trees.

She'd been a child then, with mysteries all around her, mysteries that time had made commonplace. Now, in age, she thought she might yet divine what her grandmother had heard that night. Toward twilight, sitting out on her back porch in an old rocker, she would think about it. Someday it might come to her, what it had been.

II—THE SLEEPER IN THE BARN

Every night around nine-thirty the dogs barked for a little while. Often by then Lacy was already in bed; he ignored the barking or else put his head out the back door and called, "Hush up!" in case someone was sneaking around, maybe thinking the house was empty. The house was looking somewhat neglected, he knew that, but he was doing the best he could.

He thought about the barking when his son Mitchell came and went up into the barn loft. Nobody had been up there in a year or two. Mitchell was looking for some old stuff that might be valuable now. He removed the old corn sheller and the old wheat-cutting scythe, moving cautiously down the toehold ladder that Lacy had made by nailing pieces of wood up the interior barn wall.

"You been sleeping out here?" Mitchell yelled. He thought heavy-handed jokes were what you were supposed to use with old people. "There's a bed up there. Old raggedy quilt and a pile of guano sacks on that little bit of hay. Maybe you better report it. Some tramp smoking out there could burn the place down."

"Any cigarette butts or ashes or anything?"

"Not that I noticed."

"Well. I won't bother him if he don't bother me."

He didn't know whether or not to tell his wife Rilla about the man sleeping in the barn loft. In a way he'd have been glad for the two of them to speculate about it, but it might worry her. She was already breathless enough, her words taxed and compromised. Looking her in the face, he could see the small light-haired, freckled woman of years ago, but seeing her across the room, facing another way, he would sometimes be taken aback by the sight of her taut, swollen ankles and sizable sagging frame. She'd always been one to see what there was to do and get it done; now she took her pills and did a little cooking, while he did the other chores. Now and again their daughter-in-law came from town bearing food, and cleaned the house. The small farmhouse had an old-fashioned graveled front yard, and once in a while Mitchell swept it and cut down the weed trees and scrub growth springing up around the back porch and the old garden place.

He hoped Mitchell wasn't going to take it upon himself to report the man in the barn to the law. Man? Maybe some kid who'd run away from home. Where had the quilt come from? Guano sacks for cover! Rank-smelling stuff.

He tried to remember when he'd first noticed the dogs barking at night. Quite a while back: that was as close as he could come. Now when they barked at nine-thirty or so, he didn't bother yelling at them: the fellow in the barn would know by now that there was someone in the house.

In the late afternoon he and Rilla sat on the back porch and stared out at the backyard, toward the old garden plot, the corn crib and granary. A dusty haze hung against the woods in the distance. One of them would say again that it was still too dry; they'd say again that the days were getting shorter. Occasionally a car passed out front; he listened as it went on down the road, heading toward the long slope in front of the church, a weariness in the sound as it died away.

They would discuss supper. Eat what was left of what their daughter-in-law had brought last time? What she cooked was sometimes too rich for them, but they told her it was first-rate. Perhaps tonight they would open a can of stew.

What was left to talk about? *Remember*—that was the word they used most. Remember the black snake that lived out in the henhouse, cleaning up the rats, eating an egg every day or so, till it died from swallowing a china nest egg? "Funny it couldn't tell," Rilla murmured. "Poor old snake! Oh Lord." He'd shown a neighbor the black snake, coiled on a rafter, and the neighbor said he couldn't have stood having it there. The snake didn't bother the hens, though, why should he kill it?

Rilla was getting worse, no use pretending. At night she slept propped up. She slept in the next room; they'd begun that a few years ago, when her breathing got noisier and she wanted the room warmer than he could stand it.

Some nights, though, she called him to her room in the middle of the night. She rapped on the wall with her stick, an old cut-down hoe handle, and he would come awake with a snort and go see about her. "I can't get my breath," she would whisper, and he would shake up the pillows and tug her higher on them, ask if she'd taken her medicine and if he could get her anything, then lie down on the other bed. She wanted company, and he understood why, but he didn't want to think about it for long.

One morning he caught sight of the sleeper from the barn. Up early, he saw a man going down the pasture at a brisk hike, heading for the woods. He stepped back behind the corn crib, not wanting to be seen watching, in case the man turned and looked back.

That afternoon he said to Rilla, "Mitchie said there was a bed out in the barn. Up in the loft, where he got that old stuff."

"Is that right." She was only half thinking about it.

"Yeah. Somebody's been sleeping out there. For quite a while. Well, I feel sorry for anybody sleeping with guano sacks for cover and spiders for company. But he don't bother me and I don't bother him."

"Well, that's good." That was what she said about a lot of things—an old habit, to be agreeable and hope for the best. "Mitchie used to play in the loft out there a lot. I was afraid he'd come across a snake or a poisonous spider. But he loved to play up there."

"That's right, he did."

❧

They turned in early. She couldn't hold out to stay up; anyway, it was their lifelong habit to go to bed early and rise at first light.

He wondered if she would rap on the wall tonight and call him in. There was the other question, too, the one he shied away from. It would happen some night, no use pretending. He hoped she would be asleep when it happened.

He lay in bed in the dark. The illuminated dial of the alarm clock said it was past nine-thirty. He was waiting, watching the clock hands reach a quarter to ten, growing a little uneasy. When he heard the dogs begin to bark, he was relieved: the man in the barn was back. It had become a sign for him, and he thought, as he drifted off to sleep: *it won't be tonight.*

NIGHT THOUGHTS

"There's a strange woman at your door," the woman at his door said through the screen.

He dragged himself up from the sofa, half-asleep. Maybe the woman was part of a dream. No, he'd have dreamed of someone more beautiful, someone he'd never seen before.

For he'd placed the woman. It was the woman who lived with the dentist. The dentist and his wife had divorced, and the dentist, who'd also been a jazz musician, had eventually taken up with a jazzier girlfriend, this woman—skinny and intense, with light, frizzy hair and miniature teeth. The dentist was a very good dentist, but was inclined to apologize for being one; as he fixed your teeth, he might allude to his years on the road with a well-known band, and explain that his family had urged him to go into this profession.

"I broke out," the woman was saying. "Anyway, I wanted to see your house. You can see in from the street."

"Well. Welcome." He tried to remember her name. He'd seen her at parties, but that had been a while; he remembered an eager laugh, and boots with little heels. "Sure. Look around. How's Arnie?" He was pleased that the dentist's name, at least, had come to him. Arnie Yost. Arnie Yost had had a stroke in the past year.

"That's a good question." She sank down on the sofa. "This is such a charming little house. Historic. I love it." She picked up the book that was lying open on the coffee table, the book he'd been reading before he nodded off. "Were you reading this?"

It was a book everyone was reading, and he'd rather have been found reading something else. "Oh—I usually have a bias against the bestseller stuff, but a friend told me I had to read it."

Was she even listening?—her eyes had abandoned the book and were busy taking in the room. "Aren't you going to offer me something to drink?"

"By all means. Some wine? Cup of coffee?" Quite possibly she'd had a drink already.

"I would love some coffee." She followed him into the kitchen. She took the room in, frankly and perhaps covetously; she went over and touched the Cuisinart. "Didn't you get married again?"

"Not for long, I'm afraid." He yawned, and turned the heat high under the kettle. "Are you and Arnie married?" She'd moved close to him, and he got a whiff of her perfume. Not bad.

"No. We talk about it. . . . You're a two-time loser, aren't you." She squeezed his arm, startling him. "But you have this marvelous house. And that car—I saw you out with the top down the other week."

"Yeah, I was pushing the season a little."

"Why did you split up, you and Sally?" Wouldn't Sally, his second wife, be surprised to hear that this woman knew her name? She must store up every scrap of information that came her way, pore over the local paper, the marriages and divorces and traffic offenses. He imagined her reading it in Dr. Arnie Yost's house, a frame-and-brick split-level over near the cemetery, according to Sally, though why she would know he couldn't imagine.

"It's a long story. As usual." Now she calls me at two a.m. when she's been drinking, and tells me what a bastard I am, and some night I'm going to ask her if she isn't ashamed to indulge in such cliché behavior—but why would he think of reporting this to an almost-stranger and explaining that he didn't unplug the phone because of his mother down in St. Louis? How impossible Sally had become was not something he generally talked about. The kettle was shrieking, and the woman—Beverly, that was her name, Beverly!—began to open cupboard doors, scrambling for cups—snatching the opportunity to look around further? She pulled out two mugs he seldom used.

"Were you married before, Beverly?" bearing down on the name now that he knew it.

"I'm not married *now*. Sure, I was married. Barry Klingler. From my hometown. We were just kids. An O.K. guy. But it kind of fell apart. So he went home to mother-in-law—stayed with my mother one summer before he moved to Oregon. She was glad to have him. I still hear from him once in a while. You've been around a while too, haven't you, Luke? You have any half-and-half, love? That's O.K., this is fine."

They took the coffee to the living room, and from her perch on the leather sofa she resumed her observation of the room; she was taking the place in as carefully as if she were a prospective tenant. He was trying to remember what band she'd sung with once, but couldn't; after that, she'd probably worked in some university office till she'd moved in with the dentist. Their crowds had overlapped slightly, hers a few years younger than his, and he tried a few names at random. The guy who gave the big parties in his studio on Washington Street, the tall poet who'd played basketball in France, the bar owner who'd shot a holdup man and then retired from the business.

She put down her coffee cup and said, "What ever happened to Cooper Braswell? You remember him? What a great guy!" Luke opened his mouth—he was certain he knew more about Cooper Braswell than she did—but he saw from her tender expression that she wanted to tell him about Cooper. "A lot of those people were so, oh, *assertive*, full of themselves. But he was gentle. And smart. From a really nice family back East. A damned nice guy."

"That guy still has my copy of *Under the Volcano*. Wherever he is."

She shrugged. "People do that a lot, don't they." Her face went dreamy again. "I wish I knew where he went."

Cooper Braswell: white-blond hair, and, in his memory, wearing summer clothes, white, tennis-playing clothes—big white tennis shoes, a white sweater with a vee of color. He'd gone to Yale, but didn't make too big a deal of it. He'd seemed much like the other people around at the time, people trying to figure out "who they were" and where they were headed, trying out new personas and getting carried away with it sometimes. Luke had left a bar once with Braswell and a girl and someone else, he couldn't remember who, and Braswell said he had to take a leak and stepped into the alley, barely out of sight. He remembered Braswell at a party arguing with another graduate student, late at night, sneering, "Sure, that's what *you'd* think, I had an idea how your taste ran!" He'd had too much to drink, which passed for an excuse; the woman with him had tried to drag him away.

"Alice Whitlock!" he said. That had been the woman's name—a small, boisterous woman, avid for excitement, though that night she valiantly tried to smooth things over. Remembering her might clarify Beverly's recollections of Cooper Braswell. But Beverly shook her head; she wasn't interested in Alice Whitlock or in clarifying her recollections.

"I remember dancing with him at a party, up in that studio you were talking about. Late in the evening. I remember what the music was."

He decided, cruelly, not to ask her. Cooper Braswell! The kind of guy who stood up and asked a question at the end of public lectures, one of those show-offy questions that was a mini-lecture in itself. A reasonably smart guy, basically decent. But ordinary; so very ordinary.

"He's probably teaching somewhere," he said.

"Maybe. I'll bet he's written something. Something *good!* He talked about writing a novel. But he was scholarly, too. I'm going to look him up in the library—I don't know why I didn't think of that before. Type his name into the Google—"

"Sure, why not."

She twitched, as if something hot had touched her somewhere out of sight. "I've got to *go*. He'll wonder where the hell I am—I just went out for some pop. 'Went out for cigarettes and disappeared forever.'"

"He's doing OK?"

She turned her hands over in a yes-and-no, who-knows motion. "He's getting rehab. He gets around pretty well, but he's still got some speech problems. Poor guy. He's real anxious." Tears stood in her eyes. "But I'm not going to leave him, I don't care what you or anybody says!"

Me?—I didn't say a word, he wanted to tell her. A small memory came: himself in the dentist's chair in Dr. Yost's office, Dr. Yost questioning the assistant about a mistake. It had been Luke's mistake, he'd got the day of his appointment wrong and had already said so, but the dentist had questioned the assistant rather stiffly. "Exactly what happened here?" (The assistant had been a tart young beauty who could give as good as she got.) He imagined Beverly going in the back door of the split-level near the cemetery, lugging the soda pop, and Arnie Yost—irritable with what had happened in his head, exhausted and impatient with his labored speech—grinding out, "Exactly what happened to you?"

"Sure, stick with him." He touched her shoulder. She was going; once he'd thought he might be in for a night of it. "Come on, I'll walk you to your car."

"I'm way down the block, I passed and thought about it and then I stopped. You'd have to lock up and everything, don't worry."

Out on the porch he said, "Something funny—the other night I heard a car stop out here, it was the middle of the night, and I got up and looked out. There was this couple standing in front of the car, kissing—just like that. Then they got back in the car. Stopped in the street, in the middle of the night. It was funny."

"That *is* funny. Well, thanks, love." It was a little affected, that *love* stuff—some necessary self-creation. She squeezed his hand; he got another whiff of her pleasant scent. "Bye now."

He watched her from the porch, under the porch light. A warm night; a bug, dazed from the light, batted against the wall. Not much traffic: at the college, it was the lull before the summer term began. A car passed, music imprisoned inside it, throbbing; it went on down the street, blotting out his view of the woman for a moment. There she was, though, opening the car door; he watched the inside light come on and go off, watched her pull away and make a left turn without signaling. There was something furtive and defiant in the darting movements of the small car. Poor kid, heading back to broken-down Arnie Yost, dreaming of ol' Cooper Braswell, whom she'd hardly known; making him into someone extraordinary. And suddenly he wanted to tell her about Sally. We met at an AA meeting; what did I expect? I thought she was serious about getting off it, that's what. The first days after she moved in, when they sat on at the dining room table after supper telling each other everything!—offering their pasts like presents. She'd told him how her father taught her to drive, putting her in the old car as they left the new car place, telling her to follow him home. Maybe the crazy father had made her audacious: when her first husband ran out on her (for good reason, she admitted), she started cleaning houses to shame him, though she could have found other jobs and wasn't suffering for money anyway. Now he saw her turning from the kitchen counter to put her arms around his neck with a particular grace—graceful as a dancer. Maybe I'd go back to her if I thought it'd work. If she wanted to try again. If she'd work at it. But she won't.

He turned off the porch light. It was quiet. That couple kissing out here the other night: in the glare of the headlights it had been a moment out of a play, out of a movie being shot there on the street; almost imaginary, lovely and mysterious.

He locked the front door. It was early, but Sally hadn't called in two or three weeks; she might be due, and he'd have trouble dropping off again afterwards. He turned off the downstairs lights and took the book from the coffee table. Going up the stairs, he was still thinking of the couple out in the dark street; of the unknown woman, her long hair and quick, light movements. Had they only been switching drivers for some reason, and kissed on the way? No, something had come over them, and they had stopped the car to hold one another for a minute there in the headlights.

THE DARK FORCES

The house surprised Dillon. Here, where Coral Gables and Coconut Grove merged, he'd expected a twenties stucco with a touch of decay, its white tile roof graying, set apart from its neighbors, aloof, in an overgrown yard. But the house, an assertive yellow, was a marvel of everyday perfection, the white tile roof gleaming in the harsh sunlight; it shared the general shape and mindset of the other houses on the block. He stared at it through his windshield. "Rather conventional for you, isn't it?" he said to his dead father.

His stepmother lived in the house now, *presumably alone.* Presumably alone—the thought amused him. No, there wasn't likely to be anyone else in the house: he'd heard she devoted herself completely to his father's memory. She was said to keep his study the way it had been when he was alive—a shrine. The books his father had written would be on display, and pictures of him, and pictures of the two of them. Soon he would see the shrine, even if he didn't worship at it. He wondered if any literary people, young poets, say, made a pilgrimage here. A few, perhaps. It was possible that his father's stock was going down now that he'd been dead ten years; that seemed to be how things worked. He'd never been quite top-ranked. But good; everyone said that. *Good.*

"I don't blame *her* that much," his mother had said. "She's just young and foolish and in love with the literary life. *He's* the one that ought to have better sense." But of course she did blame Susannah. Susannah had been one of his father's poetry students.

He hadn't met Susannah till a couple of years after the split. He hadn't wanted to meet her then: he was the oldest, his mother's confidant. But there was no way around it: he and his siblings must go up to the lake in Minnesota, where his father had rented a place.

Once there, he'd understood that a good deal was riding on this visit for someone—his father, Susannah? He resolved to do his duty; he would make his sister Helena and his brother Sonny at least pretend to have a good time. But it had been easy to have a good time. The water, kids in neighboring cottages, grilled steaks outside (when had his helpless father learned to do that?). He'd expected Susannah to look uneasy, on trial before him and his siblings, but she didn't. She was small and supremely self-confident. She tossed her long, streaked brown-and-gold hair and gave them cheerful, precise instructions about the water, the bugs, their duties. (He could have wished his mother to be this decisive, this confident, but with an effort did not.) Helena called her "Stepmom," teasing, and Susannah began to call herself that. "Stepmom says take your plates back to the kitchen and help yourself to ice cream." "You'd like to have a bunch to boss around all the time, wouldn't you," his father said, giving her a look so tender that Dillon hated him. It was a look stolen from his mother.

Now he swung into the driveway of the yellow house. She was expecting him.

❦

Her hair was so well cut, so pretty, that he didn't at once register it as white. White, though—that was a surprise. Early fifties, mid-fifties?—probably he'd never known how old she was. She was tan; she wore a short white dress, and small gold hoops in her ears. She stood very straight; there was something almost challenging about her firm posture. "Oh, it's been much too long!" and a warm smack on the cheek.

The cool inside was pleasant after the mid-May heat outside. She led him past a living room that looked as if its extreme order had not been disturbed lately, to a room overlooking the backyard. "What the real-estate jargon calls the 'Florida room'," she said. "He didn't accept the term. 'The back room,''the sun room'—that one's at least been around since the twenties, hasn't it? Anyway, what would you like to drink?"

His sister Helena had helped put him here. Susannah wasn't getting any younger, and what about the family things? (Not getting any younger? Oh, she'll bury us, he was going to tell Helena; she'll outlive us all out of sheer self-confidence.) Helena was afraid Susannah would bequeath the family things to some library, some university, if they didn't speak up. Their father had sent Sonny, the youngest, a bunch of books and two or three family pictures not long before he died, and he'd told Sonny, who'd been having a hard time, that he had a stash of books for each of the kids and here was his. Then his father had dropped dead reaching for his drink in a lounge in the Chicago airport.

"You get involved with family," he said to Susannah, "the years go by and you don't do the things you mean to do, see the people you mean to see. *Some time soon*—that's how it goes, we'll do it some time soon. But my mother-in-law's in Fort Lauderdale now, and we are *forced* to come down and check on her. She doesn't take proper care of herself. . . . Well, tell me how you've been."

She was fine. She had friends here: they'd been here long enough before he died to get to know the literary people, the university people. It was fine. She traveled some, and got away for the worst of the summer. "But tell me more about the family. I love your Christmas letters—who writes them, you or your wife?—or is it a collaboration? So lively. Is Sonny O.K. these days?"

"Sonny's fine. They finally found the right pill for his depression."

Maybe it had been a relief all those years ago, to have his father out of the house, though his parents' everyday lives had seemed tolerable enough. He thought of his father slugging down a cup of coffee before he headed off to an early class, red-eyed and irritable. ("Better learn to work when the sun's shining, instead of 3 a.m., sweetie," his mother said.) There was the occasional crisis, his father slamming out to the car and driving away as if forever; Dillon understood later that this was supposed to frighten his mother. Still, things rocked along; his parents laughed together about the silliness in his department at the college; they gave a party, and his father put vodka in his tomato juice the next morning. And there was an afternoon one summer when his father had come home from his office at school unexpectedly early and loaded the kids in the car to take them to a movie, *Conquest of the Planet of the Apes* (or had it been *Battle for?*). Dillon had been old enough to consider it *infra dig* to be taken to the movies with his sister and little brother; anyway, it was all rather curious, and the children whispered among themselves. "I think he feels bad about something," Sonny whispered. Sonny, big-eyed Sonny, had always been observant.

His father's departure had come about badly: he'd been in an accident late at night with Susannah in the car, Susannah driving—a collision, in fact. There was a paragraph in the police reports: the passenger, John Searcy, 42, a university professor, was treated at the hospital and released.

Dillon had hated that little story in the paper, and he thought he wasn't going to mind leaving town and going where no one knew him. He didn't complain when his mother said they were moving to her parents' in downstate Illinois; there was a college in town, and she was going back to school. The grandparents were very kind but very old. They were accustomed to eating small baked-potato-and-single-chop dinners, or else TV dinners, at five or five-thirty; his mother would cook after she got home from classes and the library and her part-time job, but often his grandmother threw together a rattlebrained, substandard meal. He and Helena tried to help, setting the table, opening the canned corn. All the grownups in the house were tired, always tired, though the grandmother struggled to rouse herself to conviviality, and sometimes played the piano and sang World

War I songs from her childhood, "The Rose of No-Man's-Land" and "It's a Long Way to Tipperary." The songs, and his grandmother's bony, heavy-veined hands seemed to Dillon dreadfully sad. Their grandfather napped a good deal; playing Chinese checkers, the kids took turns reminding him when he made an illegal move.

Later, he and his siblings had talked about the years with the grandparents—the time Sonny called the interregnum. "She cut off her hair! It was like a penance or something. Something symbolic," Sonny said. "Oh, baloney," Helena said. "She wanted it short because she was too busy to fool with that French twist any more."

The year after his parents' divorce, his father had won an important prize, thousands and thousands of dollars. His grandparents took a Chicago Sunday paper, and there was a little story about the prize in the book section. Toward evening that Sunday he said to his mother, "I see Dad won a prize."

"Yes."

Helena and Sonny were nearby, but neither cried, "Oh, what was it?" They'd all seen the story but had almost not mentioned it.

What if the prize had come a few years earlier? He remembered his mother typing theses late at night, theses and dissertations with hundreds of footnotes. "Why are you slaving over that?" his father said once. He was careless with money, and it was a while before his teaching jobs paid well. "Stop working and come to bed." Who could say why they'd split up? There was Susannah, though, you couldn't leave her out of it.

Their mother had expected to start teaching the next year, but ended up as a substitute. Later his sister Helena said, "It was money, wasn't it?—wasn't that why she married that jerk?" "She needed to show Dad she could get another man," Dillon said. "Or show herself." The man was Harry Lemons, whom they secretly called The Square—a good-looking guy with a cleft chin and a serious manner. He was willing, even eager, to take on the kids; he'd taught and coached a little himself, then veered off into selling. He was unbearably upbeat in the mornings. "Hey, hey, get that grumpy look off your face! Look cheerful, you'll feel cheerful, we'll all feel cheerful. Gotta get you out to the barber pretty soon before you turn into a hippie, or somebody thinks you're a war protestor." The war in Vietnam was still dragging on. "Some guy with hair down to his shoulders got caught by a bunch of fellows outside a bar down in Shelton the other night, and they cut his hair *for* him, with a hunting knife. Saved him the trouble of going to the barber."

Maybe marrying him had given their mother confidence, or good luck: she found a good job the next year. The mornings were hectic, his mother frantically trying to rouse Sonny, a deep sleeper and a malingerer, and get them all off to school. "If you don't get up right now," she cried to Sonny, "I'm going to give your egg to Beau!"—their dapper little mutt. Beau refused the egg; it stayed in his dish all day.

The life with Harry seemed to peak one night when his mother and Harry came home late from a party, Harry rather drunk. Dillon was awake when they came in because Sonny was sick. "That kid," Harry muttered, "always something wrong with him. I think he's a first-class neurotic."

"Don't say that!" Dillon said. "He's sick, he's got a fever, you don't know a thing about it!"

"Don't tell me what to say, buddy!" And they were swinging at one another, they bumped into the coffee table, something fell. "Stop it, stop it," his mother cried, "or I'll call the police!"

"Call them, are you crazy?" Harry puffed as they faced off, dodging the upended ashtray on the floor. Dillon retreated to the kitchen, where his mother was dialing the wall phone. He put a chair against the door; together they held it shut until the police came.

One of the cops knew Harry slightly from his coaching days. The cops picked up the ashtray and smoothed things over. "Hey, tomorrow you won't know what the fuss was all about. Better turn in, we don't want to run anybody in," and the cop who'd recognized Harry actually walked him upstairs and helped put him to bed. The other one gave Dillon some annoying and unnecessary advice.

He'd thought that would end the tenure of Harry Lemons, but his mother and Harry made up, and nobody mentioned that night; things rocked along as unsatisfactorily as ever. Dillon got an after-school job bagging groceries. There was a man with Tourette's syndrome working in the store, and whenever Dillon heard his wild shout from across the store, he felt pleasure and even a kind of relief. His mother had stuck with Harry another dozen years, then suddenly divorced him.

"Come see the study," Susannah said.

The study looked toward the backyard and the swimming pool. It was one of the most elegant small pools he'd ever seen, a rectangle of turquoise water a few steps down, banked by graceful, clipped shrubs; he stared at it while she waited to show him what mattered.

Here on a small table was the picture of his father he'd expected. But the face was not quite familiar: it was his father grown older, taken in the later years when he'd had guest stints here and there (Australia, Hawaii) and his children had not visited often. In the picture his father wore tinted glasses; there was a sprinkling of silver on his upper lip and chin. He didn't engage the camera but looked off beyond it, unsmiling and thoughtful, as if trying to remember something, two little vertical lines between the brows. "Isn't that a great picture?" she asked.

Among the immaculate books on the shelves there were smaller pictures and other oddments—pieces of coral rock, a snow globe, a small empty basket, and what might be a music box with a Russian design. On the desk were a pad of paper and a pottery jar of pens and pencils, and his last book, the collected.

"It's neater than any of the studies I remember." He smiled.

She looked at him as if he'd said something stupid. "Well, he's not here *working* in it."

She touched the basket on the shelf. "This was for urgent mail." She pointed to a larger basket on the floor. "That was for manuscripts. People were always sending him manuscripts, including people he didn't know! I begged him not to bother with them after his health declined, but he looked at every one of them. Just in case it was some real undiscovered talent, I guess."

He was looking at the books. "This first book, the small press book, that's really valuable, it's gone up astronomically. The second book—he said they were going to dispose of what didn't sell, so he bought the rest. It has some value too. I bet there're a lot of other first editions here, his friends' books.

Did he have plans about where his books were going to go? And his papers?"

"He sold some papers to the New York Public Library, that's all."

"Well. I've come begging, dearie—I could work up to this, and later you'd say, Oh, that's what he was really after. I came to see *you*, but while I'm here I want to talk about the books. Dad sent Sonny a batch not long before he died, and he told Sonny he had a batch for Helena and me. Helena's been pressing me to ask you about them. And about the family pictures—there're some we don't have copies of. Some of that stuff might cheer her up, things aren't going all that well. Maybe you knew Michael has MS."

"Her husband?—the doctor. I'm so sorry, I didn't know, I haven't heard from her in God knows when."

"She's pretty busy looking after him. And the twins are still at home." He waited. Had she even taken in what he'd said about the books?

She looked around the room. "He worked a lot late at night. Night, that's the time I can work, he said. It's when the *dark forces* come out. I imagined it like some fog rising out of the ground." Her eyes had gone dreamy: the old spell had come over her for the moment. "Once in a while he worked all night, when something was really going. Of course, he didn't have the zip for that later on."

She moved toward the door; the time in the shrine was over.

"Come on, I'll take you to lunch," he said. "I expect there're a lot of good places in Coral Gables?"

"We can eat here. There's some cold soup and some avocados and cheese and some good bread. You can help me," and he followed her brown legs and small sandaled feet into the kitchen.

❦

"She feeds me well," his father had said once. That was the summer Dillon had been taking the bus around the country, out on his own at last; he'd written a card and said he was coming (ready or not!). They had received him nicely. "She takes care of me," his father said, as if pointing out some reason for this alliance. (Who'd believe that was it?)

That visit, his father had talked to him about other poets for the first time. "So what are you reading? Yeats, Frost, that's good. So many kids don't know anything more than ten or twenty years back."

He hadn't read that much of them, but had known to give the right answers. "Mom put me onto them. And Auden. And told me to read you, too," he'd said, slyly.

"Did she. Nice of her. . . . Don't get sidetracked on the language poets, that's my advice. Stay off drugs and language poets."

He hadn't read much of his father's work yet; he would open one of the books and then balk in front of the poems, like a horse at a hurdle; he would start to read and find he was thinking of something else. But he'd forced it at last, and prepared for this chat. "That poem about the sea hare, squirting its ink—that's really nice. Where did you write that?"

His father's smile might have been slightly pained. (As if his least favorite poem had been praised?) "Oh, that was a long time ago. One of my earliest. Down in north Florida."

When he started up to the company bedroom that night, his father called, "I see you've changed the spelling of your name." It had been Dylan to start with.

"Yeah." It had been a teenage assertion of independence, of self-creation. He thought he had to offer an explanation. "People might think it was Bob, not Thomas."

"It was your mother who wanted to name you that. I wasn't that crazy about his stuff, dear old drunk that he was. Though maybe she just liked the name in general—I don't remember."

He and Susannah ate outside at a very small table, sitting almost knee to knee. The patterned sunlight, filtered through the trees, lay around them. They finished the soup; she put the bowls down on the patio floor. She seemed to take a deep breath.

"Helena ought to write me. I know you kids held it against me, that was natural. But we were right for each other! He said he didn't know how unhappy he was till he met me. Me, I couldn't bear to leave the office after a conference, I wanted to stay there forever. It was as if I'd finally found the person I'd been looking and looking for. He worried, though, he felt really bad about it—what he was doing to Eileen and you kids."

Ah, yes, Dillon thought. He did something bad and then felt really bad about it. He shrugged. "It was a while ago."

"He needed something new. The freedom! He said I stimulated him. He did some of his best work after we got together, isn't that true? I more or less gave up my own ambitions, you know, I made his life my work, my *art*. I understood what he was doing. The *imperishable* word, the imperishable line, that was what he was after. I understood that."

"Yes." Here, sitting across from her in the sun in this pretty place, he had the disorienting sense of knowing, this moment, exactly how it had been; of almost *being* his father, drawn to a new life with this woman (still remarkably good-looking) who had yearned so desperately toward him and his work. She'd never seemed to be his stepmother, even after the first angry repudiation wore itself out; she'd seemed too young and unsuited to the role, perhaps from some excess of sexual energy—or that might have been what his teenage mind imagined. "I see," he murmured. He did see! It was a kind of luxury to understand; there was a dreamlike, drowsy, almost sensual feel to it.

"We read Shakespeare aloud to each other. And we investigated new music. Oh, he taught me quite a lot." She broke off a tiny piece of bread. "Should I have brought out butter?"

"No. Well, I'm sure it was a good life." He had to be pleasant, didn't he, while he was here eating her food? Anyway, this moment with her *was* pleasant; he luxuriated in it. "Too bad he died relatively young. Compared to a lot of people now. He wasn't that sick for long, was he?"

"Um-m, several years. It could have been circulatory. He got kind of crabby and forgetful—don't you remember how he was the last time you saw him? I just sensed changes in blood flow to the heart or maybe the brain—I was just guessing. He didn't really trust doctors. And he wouldn't stop drinking. I guess he couldn't."

Astounding: she was crying. She put her elbow on the table, jiggling the wine glasses, and put her napkin over her lower face; she cried almost soundlessly.

He reached for her free hand. "I'm sorry. It was a terrible loss for you. . . ."

"He was terrible the last year or two. Simply awful—I can't tell you. The things he said to me, oh God! The things I put up with!" She was struggling to keep her wavering voice under control. "I forgave him. I took care of him, and I forgave him!"

"He wasn't himself. You were very, very important to him." He gave her hand a gentle squeeze, and let it go.

"Of *course*." Her brows went up resignedly, and she began to eat again, her eyes on the plate.

ॐ

"I'd better get on up the road," he said as they took the dishes back to the kitchen. "Diane wanted to come see you too, but when we're here she's busy with her mother, taking her places and making her do what she ought to do. She was taking her to the podiatrist this morning."

"Yes, it would have been nice to see her. About those books—let's see."

In the study she bent to a shelf that held two sections of books separated by bookends and an open space. "Take these. Wait, I'll get you a box." In her absence, he looked at the books at the other end of the shelf; he recognized the fine press book, with its rough gray paper cover; the selected, the collected; semi-rare early books by his father's contemporaries. The two little collections seemed nearly identical. His father had surely set these aside before he died.

She was back with a box, and he loaded the books into it. She went to a closet and took out a picture in an oval frame. He remembered it: his paternal great-grandparents, taken by an itinerant photographer. "Take this, you and Helena and Sonny can fight over it." Needling?—but she smiled quickly, as if to soften it. "I'll have copies made of some of the others. Do you want a copy of that one?" pointing to the big picture of his father on the desk.

He hadn't thought of wanting it, but it seemed he ought to say yes. "Why not. But we won't fight over anything. Sonny has his books, and it looks as if there's another stash there for Helena. Which I'm sure she'd appreciate." Not quite needling, in return.

"You want them for Helena? Well, O.K. I thought she might come for them sometime herself."

"As I said, she has her hands full right now." She fetched another box, and he loaded Helena's books into it.

Leaving her house, he turned toward the water; he could go back to town by Bayshore Drive.

The dark forces. A little romantic; it didn't sound much like his father's language. During one period, his father had written the children a group letter every few months—carefully written letters that sometimes spoke of literary matters they couldn't quite grasp, as though the letters were also for some unknown other person or persons. Later Dillon understood that the care that went into the letters had to do with his father's devotion to language—it would have pained him to write any other way—and the value, possibly too high a value, that he put on his own experiences. He expected the letters to be saved. Dillon regarded this calculation on his father's part with a slight disdain; but he began to save the letters.

Whenever he'd returned from a visit to his father, his mother had asked, "Well, how was it?" She asked it with a little smile that was resigned and even embarrassed, as if acknowledging that his father, at a lake resort in Minnesota, or living, another year, in sight of the water in southern California—wherever he was—held all the good-time cards.

And Dillon always said, "Oh, it was O.K. Nothing remarkable," described the house and the neighborhood, and left it at that.

His mother was still in that southern Illinois town, in a retirement complex now. During his most recent visit, he'd found her one evening reading an old anthology, leaning in toward the table lamp. She was a small, lean person now, her face somewhat weathered, tiny diamond studs in her ears. "I just re-read some Irving Kessler. Really nice poems, about his mother and his sisters—I really like them. I knew him. We liked each other, we went out together a couple of times the year I lived in New York. Maybe with a little encouragement. . . . But I might not have understood his background. I might have disappointed him in the end."

"Still brooding about the past, Mom?" Dillon said lightly.

She was surprised. "Just thinking about it. Old people do, they have time for it. You will too."

He was keyed up from being out with friends and having a few drinks, and he asked, "Did you ever forgive him—Dad?"

She looked even more surprised. "I don't know. Really, I don't. . . . I've kind of forgotten what he was like. Sometimes I remember some silly little thing, and I don't know if it was him or Harry."

Who'd believe that? It was some ancient pride—even yet, even with him! Probably her I-don't-know, I-really-don't was true, though.

Would he tell her how Susannah had suffered during his father's last years—"Aren't you lucky, Mom"? No, he'd tell her quite neutrally, and they would shrug and not say anything more. She would try hard not to be glad, but in some dark uncharted area of her being, some nearly inaccessible part of her consciousness—oh, deep in her soul!—she would see it as just. He wouldn't add that he had kissed Susannah goodbye warmly, with a feeling that mysteriously dismissed the old resentments. Already that seemed surprising; later he might feel sheepish about it.

Here was the Coconut Grove marina, the conglomeration of masts out on the water, on the other side of the road the absurdly tall apartment buildings with their stacked balconies gazing out toward the bay.

Making a turn, he heard the boxes of books in the trunk shift slightly. What he'd salvaged: the books for himself and Helena, for his mother the little sop of Aren't-you-lucky. A little something for everyone. It came to him that he'd read probably less than half his father's work. Maybe he'd catch up now. Not in the editions in the trunk, but in the everyday books on his shelves at home. Stanzas perhaps not imperishable, but good, waiting patiently all these years, hidden by so much else. He gave a small mental wince, a mental shrug. But for the moment it was all behind him, back in Susannah's keeping, and he sped along peacefully through the patchy sun and shade of the avenue.

UNFINISHED BUSINESS

The last year of their marriage, Ann and Walker Lashley sometimes spent the evening in different rooms of the house, writing to each other. Ann sat at the dining room table writing rapid longhand full of dark underlinings and exclamation points; Walker sat in his study, typing in a fierce rat-a-tat-tat. Josh, who couldn't read yet, drifted uneasily back and forth between them, making up messages for the grandmothers to whom they pretended to be writing. Some nights they hired a sitter so as to carry on the quarrel away from him. They drove around, they parked on deserted streets in front of closed business establishments. It would grow late; other people, happier people, would come out of movie theaters, get into their cars, and drive away, and Ann and Walker still would not have had it out. They saw, that year, that they never would.

After the divorce, Ann believed she'd come through it quite creditably. She'd settled business matters with Walker as quickly and agreeably as she could; she'd explained everything to Josh patiently, over and over; she'd been close-mouthed with curious friends. When Walker and one of his students came in a U-Haul truck to get his things, she put on a good show of cordiality, partly for Josh's sake; she gave them coffee and maneuvered them into taking Josh for a ride in the truck. When they left, and the high-backed truck moved clumsily off down the street, she thought with relief that it was over and that she'd behaved quite decently.

It was when she thought of Ione, Walker's mother, that it would occur to her that there might be unfinished business. She and Ione had got along well enough—not too well, not too badly. Now she wished that she had been a little nicer and Ione a little less so, so that she could write Ione off along with Walker. But why should she hesitate to do so? She'd been nicer than a lot of daughters-in-law. Ione herself was full of stories of selfish girls who dragged their husbands all the way across the country to some God-forsaken state where the girl's family happened to live, or who quarreled with their mothers-in-law and then tried to keep the husband and his mother apart. In one of these stories, the mother met her son on the sly, waiting in his car in the parking lot behind his office; she would crouch low or lie down in the back seat so as not to be seen by anyone who might report it to his wife. Whenever she told this story, Ione would begin to sob. Walker, of course, would have left the room and Ann would be *stuck* with Ione, the two of them at opposite ends of Ione's gold-threaded brown sofa, faced off like the pair of jewel-eyed seahorses on the wall behind them. The second time she heard the story (she thought of it as being *subjected* to it), Ann laughed shortly and murmured, "How romantic!" Ione was blowing her nose; she stared. "That's what *you* think!" she said hoarsely. "I just hope nothing like that ever happens to us, that's all." "Of course not, Ione," Ann said. "I wouldn't *let* it happen."

How could an intellectual like Walker take his mother seriously?—a woman who called masonry *mosonerry*, debris *derbriss*, and spoke of the prostrate gland, who awarded her vote to the handsomest political candidate, got her medical advice from pharmacists, and told you quite seriously that the best thing for an earache was a teaspoon of warm urine in the ear. Certainly her son should love and honor her, but it was hard to see how he could take her seriously. Walker did, though; he listened to the most absurd notions with a foolish patience, then some teasing criticism of himself would make him flare up. But Ann didn't think about it often: Ione lived in Charlotte, a long way from Iowa, where Ann and Walker met and were married, and a long way from California, where they split up.

Six months after the divorce, Ione wrote to Ann. She said she had cried when she heard the news. She seemed determined to share the blame, and said she hoped she hadn't brought Walker up to be selfish and inconsiderate. She'd given him a lot of attention, of course, she had wanted him to follow his star—and she believed she'd been right, judging by the reviews of his new book. (Was she apologizing or bragging?) But she was sorry, especially on poor little Josh's account.

She enclosed a letter for Josh, and five dollars. When Ann had read him the letter, they made a money belt from a cowboy belt and an old billfold, and he wore it for a week, keeping it on under his pajamas at night. The next day he said they ought to answer Ione's letter right away.

It was fall, and they were living in Iowa City, Ann's home town. She'd rented an old house and enrolled Josh in first grade and herself in library school. At first she and Josh had stayed at her parents' on Summit Street, where Walker had courted her, and she thought of him surprisingly often. How he was going to miss this street and this house! He'd admired the great arched windows that faced the side yard on two floors, had praised the lily-patterned stained glass on the front doors. When he'd first come to dinner (he'd been teaching in the Writers' Workshop at the University, where she'd been a graduate student) she'd taken him up to the attic to show him how far you could see. Perhaps if he'd known how many people in town were in love with Summit Street he'd have been less impressed, but he was attracted to its old houses, hitching posts, and overarching maples—most of all by this house. Once he'd come up to the walk while she and her mother were playing piano duets, and he had not rung the bell but sat on the steps for half an hour, listening. (Once he'd thought he heard her playing Chopin as he approached but it had turned out to be her mother instead. This emotional turnabout had interested him, and he'd written it down in his notebook.) The next year, after they were married, they'd lived in her parents' garage apartment, the second floor of what had once been a carriage house.

The house she rented for herself and Josh had a sloping front porch, small, cramped rooms, and a mousy smell in the kitchen. Still, it had touches of gingerbread, and an overgrown back yard that Josh said was full of good hiding places. (Surely it would stir a child's imagination more than their California ranch house.) There, in the breakfast nook of its sunny kitchen, Josh dictated his letter to Ione:,he could print a little but wanted this letter to be in *cursive*. He was a serious child whose laughter often came after a pause, as if it had taken a moment for him to come out of his thoughts. That morning he rose bouncily on the balls of his feet, pacing the scarred linoleum with what seemed a new authority—a nice looking child with a neat head of short brown hair, and a little ice-pink color in his cheeks. He resembled the Limoseths, her family (the Lashleys were a large, dark lot).

She took down his dictation in a large, somewhat childlike hand, to show him a good example of cursive, and to give Ione the feeling that the letter really was from Josh. He was telling Ione that he wished he still lived at his grandparents', near his friend Terry. This house was O.K., Terry came over sometimes, and they'd made a hideout under the back porch. It wasn't as good as the house in South Laguna and the TV wasn't as good here either.

Waiting for him to go on, she stared out at the backyard, where the bright leaves of October lay caught in the long silky grass, grass that should have been cut again before the leaves fell, if she hadn't been trying to save every penny. The clumps of overgrown grass, the ancient garage and its sagging doors, the moldy lilac bush—everything in and around this lopsided house was worn out and neglected. She felt a little ashamed of it, a little self-conscious, as if Ione had come in to take note of it all. Well, Ione didn't need to feel sorry for her!—she would tell Ione not to waste her tears, the divorce had been a move long overdue. She realized that Josh was waiting for her to take down the next sentence: he was inviting Ione to come and see them next summer. She wrote it down in the same large, careful hand: summer was a long, safe distance away. Anyway, Ione had waited six months to write; surely she wouldn't take them up on the invitation.

꙰

But she did; she came the next summer. At the airport she began to cry, as if they had suffered a common bereavement. She hugged them hard, shaking her head, her lips quivering.

She was a tall, thick-waisted women, with black hair threaded with white; beneath her melancholy dark eyes there were chronic circles nearly as dark as bruises. She had traveled in dark pants and jacket, wearing a man's gold wristwatch, once her husband's, and a strip of red veiling around her hair. In the car she unwound the veiling and seemed to strip off her melancholy thoughts with it. "Josh, honey, I put my travel insurance in your name. If the plane had gone down, you'd've been a rich little boy."

"I'm glad it didn't go down, Grandma," Josh said in his little tenor voice.

Ann and Josh were back at her parents' house. "Josh is happier there, that's all," she said to Ione, unwilling, for some reason to add that the crooked house had cost a fortune to heat, and that the student roomer-and-sitter she'd taken in had been a bad choice. Ione said she didn't blame Josh, she'd loved Summit Street herself when she'd visited Ann and Walker there.

What a marvelous idea this visit had been! The first few days, Ann overheard Ione telling Josh family stories—about being roused from sleep to see Halley's Comet, and seeing her cousin go off to the First World War; about Cousin Ouida Stoker, who at twenty had killed herself with Paris green, over nothing; about Great-grandpa Zach Hildreth, who jumped in the pond in his nightshirt to make the frogs stop hollering. (Did Walker tell Josh stories like that? Probably not; he was busy *using* them, and once he used them, he was through with them.)

Then, midway the week, midway her visit, Ione asked if she could see the apartment over the garage, where Ann and Walker had once lived.

"Oh, I hate to bother the Appels, the people out there, they're both in law school and terribly busy," Ann said, not pleased at the request. It seemed a bit tactless to ask to revisit what had been Ann and Walker's honeymoon cottage—how could anyone who'd cried that much at the airport bear to see it? "Anyway, it looks entirely different now."

"Oh, I see. Well, that's O.K."

But the next evening, as Ann cleared the supper dishes from the table on the screened porch, she saw a figure in dark pants and flowered tunic on the far side of the backyard by the phlox and daylilies, near the garbage cans: Ione, of course. How quietly she'd gone out, how carefully she'd observed at what hour Barbara Appel took out the garbage. While Ann watched, Barbara appeared; the two women talked for a moment then disappeared around the corner of the garage, toward the steps to the upstairs.

"She's so stubborn!" Ann said to her mother in the kitchen. Hadn't they done enough for Ione? Hadn't the beef at dinner been well-done because she couldn't stand it bloody, the angel pie made in her honor? Hadn't Ann's father taken Ione and Josh to the little town of Rochester to show Ione the rare wildflowers in the cemetery there? But it hadn't been enough: what Ione wanted was to walk through the rooms where Walker had lived nearly a decade ago. "All roads lead to Walker, he's never off her mind for long. Sometimes I thought she wanted to crawl into our skins and *be* us!"

Her mother was hurriedly rinsing plates for the dishwasher; she was going to a meeting of the city zoning and planning commission and had on her earrings and dress shoes; her expression said she would consider the Ione question impartially. "Well, you know, she's getting on up there." She was clearly not sorry to be the younger, slimmer, more civic-minded grandmother. "Why didn't you take her on out there—how could they have refused?"

"She hasn't come to see *me*, maybe not even Josh, she's come to see Walker's son and his son's mother—"

"And of course you invited her for the pleasure of her company," her mother said, dropping her voice as Ione came up the back steps.

Making her escape, she found her father in the living room looking alert, the evening paper slack in his hands. Behind his steel-rimmed glasses his eyes were questioning. She sat down on the hassock by his feet and smiled, almost sincerely. "It's nothing important Daddy. She wanted to see the apartment and I should've taken her out there, I should have known she'd see it or bust."

Her father shook his head. "She's nice, but she's hard-headed." He chuckled somewhat maliciously. "Over at Rochester yesterday we got to talking about birds, and we got into evolution—Josh was telling her some things, and she said 'I don't believe a word of it.' I tried to tell her I didn't think evolution was totally incompatible with Christianity, but I could tell she wasn't going to take it in." He spoke softly, but with an odd vehemence, and she suspected that he was really thinking of Walker. He'd insisted on talking books with Walker, and there'd been a time when she'd thought she'd better speak to each of them about it in private. "Well, he can disagree with me all he wants to," her father had said, "but he ought to be polite about it. Maybe he doesn't *know* Ole Rolvaag or Hamlin Garland, they're another generation, but he ought not to smile like that." When she gave Walker a watered-down version of this, he said he didn't know he'd been smiling; but he shook his head. "I can't tailor my opinions to fit the occasion. You'd think he'd be interested in *my* opinions—I teach courses in fiction! But he wants me to agree with him."

"Really, it's nothing, Daddy," she said now. "And she's having a really good time. You and mother have been really nice."

But that was talk meant for her father. The next day she woke up to find old grievances come to life overnight. "What an insane idea, to invite her!" she muttered to her mother. "You know what I woke up thinking about? The time she asked Walker which of us he would save if we were in a boat that was sinking."

"Oh, isn't that some old joke?" her mother said.

"Why didn't he treat it like one then!" The night Ione asked that silly question, asked it twice, to rouse him from his newspaper, Walker had muttered, after a long pause, "I'd let you both go down." Ann had stared at him indignantly; Ione had laughed a guttural laugh, as if willing to be insulted as long as Ann was insulted too. Ann had taken it up with Walker that night in their bedroom, in case there was something she hadn't understood, but Walker only groaned and said it was so awkward when she and his mother started fighting over him; surely she could see that he was stuck in the middle. "I wouldn't fight over anyone!" she exclaimed, but Walker's voice got louder, threatening a quarrel, and since his mother was the last person she wanted to overhear one, she had had to let it go. Oh, she was right to have divorced him, she was *glad* to have divorced him, and why hadn't she divorced his mother at the same time?

Those recollections put her in a bad humor, but Ione was in a wonderful mood the rest of the week, as if seeing the apartment had given her a deep satisfaction. Whenever she won a struggle she was likely to do some troublesome and unnecessary good turn for whomever she had bested, and it was no surprise that she insisted on mending a nasty three-cornered tear in Ann's new silk blouse, and, for good measure, strained her eyes helping Josh put together his six-hundred piece model of an aircraft carrier. Then, at the end of the visit, there was a morning of presentations: Ione gave Josh her father's drawstring money bag and some Indianhead pennies and silver dollars, and gave Ann her grandmother's sampler and garnet ring.

"It's sweet of you, Ione, *thank* you, but it's too much, really," and when Josh was out of hearing Ann added, "You know, Walker may very well marry again and have more children, and you might wish you'd saved some of these things." She was glad to have an occasion to show Ione that she thought of it all quite matter-of-factly.

Ione's face went gloomy. "I don't care! That's his business. I'd love any kids he had, but Josh was the first, nobody could ever take his place." She waited a moment. "And you were the first wife, too, that's something nobody can ever take away from you."

"Goodness, who on earth would want to?" Ann said.

❧

Each summer it was a question: how to get Josh to California for his summer visit with Walker. Once a friend of Ann's on her way to the West Coast escorted him; once her parents combined the duty with a vacation. But the next summer, Ione made a suggestion: she could come for a visit, and then accompany Josh to California, with Walker footing the bill. They were several years into this convenient arrangement before Ann realized it was going to make Ione's visits irreversibly annual.

Walker could afford to foot the bill. His latest novel was reviewed everywhere and nominated for prizes; his face, darkened by an unfamiliar beard, smiled his familiar, uneasy smile at her from *Newsweek* and the book page of the Sunday *Des Moines Register*. Josh got postcards from New York and Colorado and Arizona when Walker gave readings or went to a writers' conference. He'd had a Guggenheim, money from the National Endowment, awards she'd never heard of before. He'd married again, a former student named Bernadette, and soon Josh came back from visits with pictures of himself cheerfully holding the baby.

"Bernie was raised a Catholic," Ione said impressively, as though that were unusual, "but she's not one now. I don't guess she's *anything* now. She's a pretty girl, but I just about starved out there. Alfalfa sprouts, bean sprouts, all kind of sprouts! Whenever I was out by myself I'd get me a hamburger. But she's crazy about Walker and I guess he is about her too."

Was she saying that Walker had found the right person this time? Sometimes Ann felt the bright beam of Ione's curiosity playing over her, Ione wondering exactly how friendly she and Walker were now. Well, they were friends, but not close friends. The letters they wrote to arrange Josh's visits had grown a little longer; Walker sent news of friends in California, and she wrote him her own good news, about her trip to Spain with her parents and Josh, about the law professor she was about to marry until she changed her mind, rather late. (Not the least of what she held against Walker was the fact that he'd spoiled a lot of people for her; listening to them, she'd think of the way his lips moved as he said *idée reçue*.") And how friendly did he feel? He'd put her name in *Who's Who*—not all first wives made it—but perhaps on Josh's account. When he learned she was buying a house because her parents were moving south, he'd offered to help, which reminded her that he was in the money while she was living on a high-school librarian's salary— not that that was Walker's fault, exactly, but how could you calculate the cost of a ruined marriage? Of course the marriage had been an error in judgement on both sides. Walker, misled by her Chopin and her delicate blonde prettiness, had thought she was softer and more malleable than she was; she too had been misled, charmed by his teaching and his first book; she'd got him and his book all mixed up together. There was a lot she hadn't noticed right away, such as his haphazard manners; perfectly routine politeness sometimes seemed to strike Walker as a sign of weakness. And how could she have guessed, dazzled by his book, that while he worked on the next ones she would be at pains to keep Josh quiet, taking him on long excursions, hoping always for good weather? "Can we go home now?" Josh asked plaintively down on the beach one chilly afternoon. "Will it bother Daddy if we go home now?" Not that it was Walker's fault that he needed quiet to work; but it had been awkward, and they'd complained back and forth. Once an argument had nearly flared on Christmas Day. "Not fussing on Christmas!" Josh said with a soft groan. Maybe that was the day she decided it was hopeless. That was a long time ago, and now Walker was offering her money toward a house. In the end she declined his offer, but with a very polite thank-you.

❧

Ione came in the spring of Josh's thirteenth year; he was old enough now to make the summer trip to California alone. It was during this visit that Keith Causey called.

"A man called—the nicest man!" Ione said, meeting Ann at the door when she came in from work. "Keith Causey!"

"Who?" Ann leaned around Ione to call hello to Josh, who was shuffling cards at a card table in the living room, where he and his grandmother had been playing Crazy Eights.

"He's a friend of Walker's, passing through. He called from somewhere out on the road, and he's going to come out tonight."

"He is!" Ann cried, stepping out of her damp boots. It had been a day of wild, restless weather, a wet spring morning followed by a windy afternoon that was rapidly turning colder. "Honestly, aren't people nervy, though, inviting themselves out—"

"Oh, no, honey, I invited him. He was so nice, he knew who I was, and he says he knows you too. He's been on his spring break, and he's on his way back to Colorado, he teaches out there."

"Keith Causey! I certainly don't place him. And I thought I might do some work tonight."

"Oh. Well, I didn't know what to say. I thought you knew him, a little bit, anyway. He's writing a book about Walker."

"A book about Walker? Really. Are you sure it's not just an article?"

"He said it was part of a series—he told me the name but I've forgotten."

Josh got up and strolled around, listening. He'd grown taller in the past year and had a loose-kneed walk, as if he might suddenly leap to catch a fly ball; long lashes gave his small-featured face a delicate quality. Walking around the room, he fingered the pencils and pens in the Keiller jam jar on the wicker desk, looked among the dried fronds in the vase on the bookcase, peered past the open wing of the piano into its depths, and silently touched one or two of its keys. "Don't you think he could have a whole book written about him some time? He's had a lot of prizes, and he's in a whole lot of anthologies," he said in a tone of cheerful persuasion.

"Oh, of course, I just meant now, that's all."

Ione had been listening to Josh with a look of happiness; turning back to Ann, her face drooped. "You don't want to fool with it! I'm sorry, I didn't know you had work you had to do."

"Oh, it's not really that urgent." It was a booklist for the newsletter at Josh's school and it wasn't due for ten days; still, Ione had made rather free with her evening. A friend of Walker's! How close a friend could he be if he thought Walker's name gave him instant entrée here?

"It's all right. Of *course* you want to meet him."

She'd met him before, after all. When the knocker banged and she saw him through the glass by the front door, she knew she'd expected someone that size and shape, someone like the bearded man in the duffel coat who stood under the porch light, his high forehead exposed to the cold wind. She opened the door with a smile meant to hide all she couldn't remember, and Keith Causey came in with a gust of cold air, saying, in light-hearted apology, "I seem to have brought winter back."

He held her hand longer than necessary, and told her she hadn't changed at all, and that this was very kind of her. He declared that he'd have known Ione anywhere, she and Walker were so much alike. As he talked, she remembered that he'd come to do an interview with Walker for a little magazine, out in California. He hadn't changed much, though his dark curly hair began farther back; hair and beard encircled a face that looked younger than it probably was, with its wide-eyed, taking-in gaze. Why had she forgotten him? But she'd seen him for only a few minutes when he'd come for the interview, then she and Josh had left the house. It had been a year of quarrels—plenty of other stuff to forget.

Ione went to get coffee, and Keith Causey turned to Ann. "I was going to call again after you got home and make sure this was all right, then I decided maybe I'd better let well enough alone."

They both laughed. "Oh, it's fine, really," Ann said. "Ione says you're working on a book about Walker."

"Yes. He's seen some of it. He seems to think it's O.K."

Ione, coming back with a tray, said, "That's wonderful! I'll bet it's good, and I hope I have the opportunity to see it sometime." She put down the tray; winking at Ann, she ran her finger down the sleeve of his jacket. "Let me touch you— maybe some of that *smart* will rub off on me."

"I've been studying his work for quite a while. I staked out my claim early."

Ione smiled warmly. "Well, that's great. I guess it helped for you to be out there near him—too bad you've left there."

"Where were you?" Ann asked. "San Diego? It's nice. Did you know the Lohrmanns?"

Ione leaned forward in her chair. "Mr. Causey—well, *Keith*—Ann has some work she has to do, I didn't know it when you called. I know you won't mind if she goes and does her work."

In the end, she had to go; it would be awkward to explain that most of the work had to be done at the library, and that he'd kept her from going out. "Well, half an hour then. And I'll call Josh, he wants to meet you."

ৡ

"I know you've heard him mention Cheeke," Ione was saying downstairs in the living room.

"I know a great deal about Cheeke. The Goodnights and Stoneys, and Mary Queen Somebody—"

"Mary Queen Williams. Walker loved that town! We went there when he was four and everybody always made a big to-do over him. Alton, my husband, was principal there. You wouldn't believe how different it all was back then! The principal's house was right on the school grounds, and we had our chickens in a pen down in the woods. . . ."

In the upstairs hall Ann stood listening. She'd heard the front door open and close. Keith Causey had gone out for a few minutes and returned, then he and Ione had gone on talking. It was still too soon to go back down.

"But my husband's health failed and we left there. He was in a sanitarium for a while, and Walker and I went and stayed with Alton's father, he was a widower and needed somebody to keep house. . . ."

Ann tiptoed back to her room. Ione was prettying up the Lashleys' history, but who could blame her? The sanitarium

Walker's father had gone to had been a place for alcoholics. He'd been able to hide his drinking till one commencement day when, handing out diplomas on the stage of the school auditorium, he'd begun to mix up the names. They came out funny, as funny as some of the remarks he made to the seniors who filed past. "What does a pretty girl like you want with this little piece o' paper?. . . . Well, here's one I never expected to see up here, but you made it, didn't you, ol' buddy. . . ." Whispers ran through the audience, and a few guffaws; Ione began to cry. She told the people around her that he had a terrible toothache and had taken some whiskey for it, which was *true*, she said when she told Walker about it years later. Walker had come to think it tolerably funny, and sometimes told the story of the last commencement. Once when Ann had tried to get him to tell it, though, he'd clammed up.

When she went down to the living room, Keith Causey and Ione smiled silently; they were listening to a tape he'd just made. "He wanted to *record* me," Ione said with self-conscious pleasure when he turned it off.

"What a good idea. Let me see where Josh has got to."

She found him watching television in the basement rec room, and when she appeared he sighed but got up. "I thought you were interested in this man," she murmured as they went up the stairs, Josh taking them three at a time.

"Sure. But he was taping it all and I couldn't think of a whole lot to say."

"Well, I think he's finished now. Having preserved your grandma for posterity."

Keith Causey asked who played the piano. Then he asked Josh if he wanted to be a writer too. Josh, looking at Ann, said probably not; but maybe so. Ann said Josh was interested in science; his genetics project had won second place in the school science fair. Josh frowned at her warningly. Soon he excused himself; the refrigerator door slammed, and his footsteps sounded on the basement stairs.

"Ione, I'm really indebted to you for this tape," Keith Causey said. "But I don't want to wear you out. I'd like to take a quick look around town. Maybe Ann will come with me, show me the significant landmarks."

"You're not wearing me out," Ione cried. "Goodness, I don't go to bed this early! Stay as long as you like, you don't have to go!"

With disappointment, almost disapproval, she watched him hold Ann's coat. "I'm sure glad you came, it's meant a lot to me," she said. Keith kissed her cheek and said he might pass through Charlotte some day and would certainly call her. But her dark-circled eyes stayed melancholy as they said goodnight.

"Isn't she a sweetheart!" Keith Causey said in the car. "You must get along pretty well, though I assume it's a grandmotherly visit. But I gather you and Walker get along well enough, as far as that goes."

"Well enough, yes."

"I'm aware that Walker wouldn't be the easiest person in the world to live with. I think he still amazes Bernie sometimes. Every so often she and the little girl go take a breather with her folks in Huntington Beach. It's been touch and go a few times, mostly go."

Was this gossip a little present for her? "She's been nice to Josh, that's all I know." She heard the excessive dignity in her voice, and relented. "Well, Walker fancies himself a father. He's good at reading them fairy tales. He and Josh get along fine now, of course."

"Before I forget, did your folks live in this neighborhood? When you and Walker lived at their place?"

She directed him to her parents' old house, and he turned into the driveway. Out in the garage apartment the lights were on and the blinds up; a hanging plant filled one window. He stared at it longer than she'd expected.

Downtown, he asked where Walker had lived before they were married. The building had been torn down during urban renewal, and she pointed out the vacant lot. "Well, well. Well, let's have a drink if you can spare the time. You'd better pick the place."

In the bar he asked if he might phone a couple he knew. "Former students of mine, here in the Writers' Workshop now. Really very talented people—you might enjoy meeting them and they'd love to meet you."

The couple, the Dineens, arrived as rapidly as if they lived around the corner. They were nearly the same medium height and wore blue down jackets and hiking boots. They hurried in and told Keith it was wonderful to see him, and their eyes swept over her eagerly.

"This was your lucky day," Gary Dineen said. "Finding his mother here too, what luck!"

The Dineens began to tell Keith Causey about Iowa City. They had funny stories about the writers who'd taught here, and Keith trotted out his own literary anecdotes in exchange; she corrected the facts in one of them, and they gazed at her respectfully. Lynn Dineen asked, "How old is your son now?"

as though she thought of Josh often. They were taking her in, memorizing her: they'd tell their friends that they'd met Lashley's first wife. Leaving, Gary Dineen made her a little bow and said, "What a pleasure to meet the real Malinda."

After the Dineens were gone, Keith Causey moved closer, his arm hooked over the back of his chair. They spoke at the same time. "Did you read—" he began.

"Who's Malinda? Is she in the last book? Well, she's not me, and I'm not her! What a nerve. He sent the book, he always sends them, but I told Josh he wasn't old enough for it, and he isn't, from the reviews I saw, and so I didn't want to be sitting around reading it. Maybe sometime. He used to read from whatever he was working on. At odd moments, when I was trying to settle the baby down for the night—" She made her laugh cheerful. "Probably Bernie has learned how to handle that." She didn't want to hear whether Bernie had or not. "Well, my father thought he was a character in one of them, but I wasn't so sure."

"Did he and Walker get along? I can imagine that for all his virtues Walker might not be the easiest son-in-law in the world to have."

"Oh, they got along fine at first. I even thought Dad was sort of a father substitute, really. Walker's father had been dead a while, and he was gone a lot when Walker was growing up—you know, off getting dried out. They had a rough time for a while, back there with Grandpa Lashley."

"Ione mentioned that, going to stay with him. What was he like?"

"Oh, he sat out on the front porch all day and didn't say much, which was lucky for them. He was quarrelsome— he sued somebody over a property line and lost, money he couldn't afford to lose. Walker said when he met somebody new at school he wasn't in a hurry to take them home, afraid Grandpa would start in and say the wrong thing about somebody's family. But he was decent to Walker and Ione, and Ione got a job in the drugstore eventually. They had to turn out the lights about nine every night to save on the light bill—Walker read in bed with a flashlight, the way my mother did at boarding school a long time ago. But his dad came back from the cure and got a job putting signs on billboards, and things got better. I'm not sure if his cure ever quite took—he'd go off on a spree once in a great while. Whenever he started drinking Ione would hide the money, and one night they started quarreling over it, and Walker was scared and waked his grandfather. Grandpa would just threaten to put them out of the house whenever there was any trouble—he was old and excitable and contrary."

"Walker'd have been nine or ten?"

"Around that. I wonder if it didn't leave him with a chip on his shoulder. But Ione knew how to program him for success! He was supposed to make the world sit up and take notice. Sort of his blessing and his burden. Actually, I'd like to know how she did it," with a little laugh. (Was that smugness in his smile?—certainly he was taking it all in.) "But how did I get into all this?"

"I asked you some questions. I'm very much interested in Walker's life, it's my job to be interested. So when did they move to Charlotte—before he started high school? His father got back into teaching, didn't he?"

"Yes. The old man died and there was a little money, and they went to Charlotte, and through some miracle he got a job teaching high school, and held onto it. Isn't it amazing how well they came out of all that! Ione is strong, she really is. It's amazing."

"It is, it is indeed."

She said she ought to be getting home. Outside there were traces of light, grainy snow on the ground, but the wind had whipped it off the sidewalks. On the way home she asked Keith Causey questions about himself without paying much attention to the answers. Displeasure with the evening was coming over her.

At her house a light showed in Ione's room. She'd be in bed, reading, perhaps *Downstairs at the White House*; her clothes, turned wrong side out, would be airing on a chair. At the front door Ann told Keith Causey goodnight. He thanked her; she wished him a good trip.

She awakened the next morning to harsh thoughts of him. Foolish of Ione to invite him out; foolish of herself to go out with him and talk too much. At least he hadn't recorded her.

She lay on in bed, occupied with thoughts of Walker, the residue of last night's talk. How careful and informed his opinions were, how staunchly unswayed by hype and fashion. How often she'd relied on them, how often she'd echoed them! And were these generous thoughts a kind of apology for last night?

Well, if Walker turned out to be as important as people seemed to think, wouldn't everything that had happened to him be in the public domain? There'd be a few people back in those little towns who remembered the Lashleys, whether Ione and Walker liked what they remembered or not. Everything she'd said was true, and what difference did it make anyway, after all this time? And it hadn't been her fault that Keith Causey had been there asking questions; if it had been up to her, he'd never have come!

"Oh, I don't know. Not too well in the end, I guess," Ann said, running some water into a pan. "He could certainly ask the questions, couldn't he. He came for some information, that's all."

"Goodness, if he writes about Walker of course he's going to ask questions!" Ione said indignantly. She came and stood by the stove, as if to put herself firmly in Ann's line of vision, though perhaps it was in order to hear better. "I liked him fine, I'd have been glad to talk a lot more, you could have finished your work—and I bet I could have told him a lot more he'd have been interested in! Well, I thought you must have liked him, you stayed out so late. I had to get up to go to the bathroom, that's the only reason I noticed. And honey, you forgot to tell Josh goodbye and when you'd be back—"

"I know, I certainly should have, but he was lost in TV land, and you were here—"

Ione smiled knowingly. "You were in a hurry to get going. Mr. Causey was a good-looking fellow! But don't forget to tell Josh where you're going when I'm not here, and I'd tell him to lock up good."

"Don't worry, I've always been careful with Josh, careful to a fault! Walker thought so, anyway. He'd put up with any old sitter as long as we got one, but if I couldn't find someone good I'd stay home—then he'd sulk. Not that it took much to bring that on!"

Ione's big, dark-shadowed eyes stared at her defiantly. "Well, I raised him the best way I knew how, just like you're doing!" Her face crumpled as she began to cry. "And I did it alone a lot of the time!" She was talking through her sobs, a moaning sound rather like the noises of the dumb. "I can't help it that he's the way he is."

"Oh, Ione, I'm sorry, don't pay any attention to me, I'm not awake yet." She patted Ione's shoulder; she was hoping Josh couldn't hear them upstairs. "And don't worry about Walker, he's doing fine."

Ione blew her nose. "I'm afraid he'll break up with *her* sometime, they've had some ups and downs. I don't like Bernie as well as I did, but still. . . ." She shook her head.

"He won't lack for companionship, believe me." For Ione, Keith Causey had been a reminder of Walker's success; she herself was a reminder of his failure. Probably Ione had imagined a different future for him—a county superintendent of schools, say, coming by with his wife and children for dinner after Sunday School—and, Ione might have cried, wouldn't he have been better off? At least as well off as he was out in California with his second family, associating, no doubt, with those unhappy people he wrote about! The clippings about himself that Walker sent gave her far more pleasure than his books.

Ione's lower lip stayed petulant. She hadn't forgotten last night, when Ann had taken Keith Causey away. Ann said, uneasily, "The Coffee's done, Ione, don't you want some?"

Upstairs, the bathroom door slammed: Josh was up. Josh, on whose account their friendship, such as it was, had endured—or that was what both of them would have said. Probably it was other unfinished business that had held them together, though. Maybe, if it hadn't been for last night and this morning, she might soon have had the account settled, and closed the books on Ione—was that possible?

"I was thinking last night, maybe Josh would like to come down and see *me* next time," Ione said. "For a change—"

"Oh, Ione, you have to come, you love Iowa City, and you always say it does you good to get away! Maybe he'd like to go back with you for a while, but you *have* to come. I'd feel terrible if you didn't." How true; truer than ever this morning.

Ione smiled shyly. "Well, I hear our boy up. I can fix his breakfast—I expect you want to get going pretty soon."

"That would be nice. I'd better get moving. Thanks a lot, Ione." Going upstairs to get ready for work she thought, with mingled relief and regret: till death do us part.

ESSAYS

ON JEAN JUSTICE'S "DOUBLE FIRST COUSINS"

Mary Szybist

Lately, when I think of Jean Justice, I think of three things she said to me.

In the mid-nineties when I was first getting to know her, I offhandedly recommended a weekend sale at a local clothing store. "We have all our clothes," she said dryly.

During one of our last visits in the fall of 2014, I asked who she relied on now to read and respond to her drafts. I don't remember her exact words, though she stated them plainly. Everyone whose opinion she trusted was dead.

In the last decades of her life, Jean seemed to have an acute sense of living in her own end times. She had a refined sense of style, evident in her clothing, in the sleek, mid-century modern feeling of her home with its selective vintage touches—a low, beautifully ornate coffee table in an otherwise spare and spacious room by a wall of windows overlooking the Iowa River. It was strange to me that she would lose interest in adding items to her wardrobe for variation, or just for the pleasure of the new. Perhaps she had a sense of sufficiency; but I suspect that she was focusing her attention on what mattered to her. She lived for nearly another 20 years. I don't know if she ever purchased another item of clothing.

I couldn't imagine writing without anyone I trusted to turn to. It struck me as lonely and also filled me with awe. Clear on the kind of stories she wanted to write, and without anyone else to help her toward them, she was remarkably prolific late in her life. If she hadn't already become one long ago, she must have become, by necessity, a writer who felt she could trust herself.

I remember another evening (this must have been sometime in the late 90's or early 2000s, when Don was still alive) she was on her way to the kitchen after dinner to bring something back for everyone, and murmured, in her wonderful Jean way, in a low, dulcet, almost coquettish tone, like she was sharing a secret, "I'm mad for something sweet."

These three notes seem to me to run through Jean's story "Double First Cousins." The challenge she gives her protagonist and narrator, Marguerite, isn't to gather insight or material for the future, but to work out a relationship to what she has: her past. She "has all her clothes." There's no one left for Marguerite to turn to for company, let alone insight. She's the only one who can re-write her story into a truer version. And pulsing through Marguerite is desire: "I'm mad for something sweet."

"Double First Cousins" is a story of how books can hurt you. How they can confuse you. How they can seduce you into wanting certain kinds of sweetness, believing they are possible; that they *are* sweet; that they are worth having. Marguerite explains,

> Gwen [her double first cousin and closest friend] and I lived in books and imagination: we read Agatha Christie and dreamed of the Calais coach and the Orient Express; of New York, where the women in magazine stories lived, owed their furriers, remembered boarding school at St. Cloud, and received telegrams and flowers. We weren't like my high school friend, Mary Alice, who'd married a hard-working, loud-mouthed dairy farmer, but even with the work and early rising finished a book or two a week; she read them fast but didn't dream over them. She'd grasped something important: that her life had nothing to do with anything in books, a distinction Gwen and I had been careless of.

The jagged terrain of the story is regret. It isn't clear that Gwen is cognizant of the affair that her huspand Kip has with Marguerite after Marguerite moves in "to help" after Gwen's diagnosis of multiple sclerosis. It is even less clear that Gwen finds any solace in Marguerite's company. In retrospect, the details of the affair interest Marguerite so little that they are almost entirely stripped from the story. Marguerite, now "an old woman," is haunted by how invisible Gwen had been to her. Justice's story is a kind of antidote to the imagination that led Marguerite to that betrayal. After Gwen's Christmastime wedding, a cousin says to Marguerite that it must make her think about when she'll get married, but it doesn't. "How could I ever match this wedding?" Marguerite thinks. She imagines "them lounging in each other's arms, by firelight, dreamy and perfect, as in a magazine illustration." Marguerite did what the books she loved encouraged her to do: participate in someone else's story.

Marguerite enters Gwen's story but is unwilling, or unable, to accept Gwen's version of it. Gwen is distraught over her diagnosis, but it is Gwen's boredom that Marguerite worries most about, which she can't distinguish from her own. "She needs me," Marguerite explains to Gwen's mother-in-law. "It's pretty dull for her down here." The romances Marguerite knew didn't prepare her to become interested in the point of view of a sick wife, but they were excellent in developing her ability to sympathize with a wealthy man, excellent at cultivating a desire for him to occupy the dramatic center. "When Kip came into a room," she explains, "he took charge, and you knew interesting things would start happening and your life would be different for at least a little while." She and Gwen could do things for themselves, but looking at art or birds or listening to music "was better when Kip was in charge." "I wanted to know what he thought about everything," says Marguerite. She had no such curiosity about Gwen. What she remembers "about Gwen's physical condition that winter is chiefly what Kip said about it." It is only from the distance of time, returning to these memories, that Marguerite is finally interested in Gwen's perspective.

Marguerite's failure on this count is the betrayal that most haunts her. And it's within Marguerite's haunting that Justice does her work, work that has something to do with investigating the idea of closeness. Marguerite begins the story,

Twice today my life was spared. The first close call was at the river bridge, when I was making a left turn. I'd misjudged the speed of the oncoming car and was barely out of the way in time; he blasted me with the horn. The sound spread out on the air, flat and metallic. I had a brief palpitation, a feeling like a small bicyclist deep in my chest, pedaling too fast, whirling away. If there'd been a crash, I'd have said to the police: my fault, all my fault!

One meaning of a "close call" is an occasion of a referee making a call that could go either way. When Marguerite was young, she understood her story one way. Now she is reviewing it, making different assessments. Marguerite may be invested in claiming fault, but that's not what interests Justice. The story is an exploration into the complicated ways we imagine and pursue "closeness"—and by beginning with a just-missed car crash, she begins by alerting us to danger: it's a straightforward example of how getting "close" risks the possibility of disastrous collision.

"Close": how strange that this word we have for intimacy is the same word we have for closure, for blocking, for covering, for ending. It also means: to bring together, the way a jaw closes. This story faces the strangeness of what seems to be the same but isn't; of what seems related, but isn't; of what seems closed, but isn't.

And yet things often *are* strikingly similar. A parallel moment to the opening car crash happens "the night everything fell apart," when, in the face of Gwen's spiraling despair, Marguerite takes Kip's side and then can't do anything but wait for her heart to stop pounding. This is the crash that wasn't averted. When people praise Marguerite for helping out, she responds, 'Wouldn't you do the same for somebody that close to you?" In retrospect, the claim of closeness seems deluded, and yet as double first cousins, Gwen and Marguerite have long been closely related by blood and proximity. Their parents were two sisters who had married two brothers; they grew up down the road from each other. That Marguerite can't always distinguish Gwen's preferences and desires from her own seems to have something to do with her inability to hear her. "You're crazy about him," Marguerite replies after Gwen voices a long series of complaints about Kip that clearly show she isn't. "Anyway," Marguerite reasons, "it had to be true; anyone would love Kip." I don't know another story that so persuasively, so unnervingly makes real how easy it is to mistake one closeness for another.

Visiting Gwen in her care home in her last years, Marguerite tells her, "I've missed you so much!" By this time Marguerite also understands how much she "missed" Gwen—missed perceiving who Gwen had become, missed the signs that could have told her "what [Gwen] was going through." It also strikes me that by moving a long geographical distance from Gwen and Kip, Marguerite "missed" Gwen through those years in the sense of sparing Gwen other ways she may have continued to collide into her, into her marriage.

How close can we really get to other people? In this story, Justice's answer seems unaccountably sad.

And yet, and yet. Marguerite *does* find her way out of the distancing frame, the story she to some degree chose to be seduced into. It's almost as if she was seduced by the sound of her own name. Among names like Gwen, Kip, Norris, and Bertha, *Marguerite* sounds out of place. Gwen is short for Guinevere, the legendary queen, and the shortening of the name fits Gwen. Her ability to see her life in a romantic framework was cut short by her illness. Marguerite has to do the slow work herself, and it takes her longer to distinguish between the fictional and the real, and to stop imagining herself as exceptional. Marguerite sounds as French as it is, though it refers to the common daisy flower.

I also find myself thinking of another Marguerite, the one from Paul Celan's "Fugue of Death." I'd be surprised if Justice didn't know the poem. I remember the lavender spine of *Another Republic: 17 European and South American Writers*, edited by Charles Simic and Mark Strand, occupied a central location on her bookshelf. Spinning throughout Christopher Middleton's translation are Margarete and Shulamith, two female figures yoked together in the poem's swirling bewilderment: "your gold hair Margarete/ Your ashen hair Shulamith." More than the doubleness of the cousins, it is the doubleness of Marguerite that comes into focus in the story, her deep capacities for blindness and insight, for indifference and compassion.

There's something beautiful in Marguerite's ability to finally step out of old narrative trappings and into a truer bewilderment. It's a vision that at least one kind of closeness is achievable: our ability to get closer to ourselves, to the truth of who we have been. The new intimacy that Marguerite forms with herself in this self-knowledge feels more true and real than any of her other relationships.

And yet, and yet. Justice doesn't end the story with the achievement of insight but in the more delicate realm of memory. Marguerite remembers a night when she and Gwen were girls, the August night of a Perseid shower when they lay on quilts in the backyard and watched stars fall. "For us back then the stars were not masses of ionized gas whirling in fiery turbulence, but beautiful fixed points that once in a while lost their moorings in the heavens and streaked down the sky." The narrative sense of self that each cousin will go on to be unmoored from hasn't yet come into view. What they share is the experience of looking beyond themselves, gazing up, side by side, at the same night sky. They aren't trying to get closer; they're in no danger of colliding; they are falling asleep together. It is this vision of closeness, such as it is, that Justice offers as possible, the closeness of these cousins in this yard, on this night, as they share a fiction about stars. Philip Larkin ends his poem "Talking in Bed" with the admission,

Nothing shows why
At this unique distance from isolation
It becomes still more difficult to find
Words at once true and kind,
Or not untrue and not unkind.

At the story's close, Justice finds those words.

MARY SZYBIST is most recently the author of *Incarnadine*, winner of the 2013 National Book Award for Poetry. Her previous poetry collection, *Granted*, was a finalist for the National Book Critics Circle Award.

THE LAST LINE

Christian Schlegel

Don Justice died in August 2004. Jean Ross Justice published
"The Dark Forces" in *The Yale Review* in 2005.

In the story's opening scene, Dillon arrives at a house
in Miami, where his father, the professor-poet John Searcy,
lived with his second wife, Susannah. She'd once studied
under John—their relationship began in scandal, though it
slowly attained respectability. Still in the car, he rehearses
for himself what he'll find inside:

> She was said to keep his study the way it had been when
> he was alive—a shrine. The books his father had written
> would be on display, and pictures of him, and pictures
> of the two of them. Soon he would see the shrine, even
> if he didn't worship at it. He wondered if any literary
> people, young poets, say, made a pilgrimage here. A few,

perhaps. It was possible that his father's stock was going down now that he'd been dead ten years; that seemed to be how things worked. He'd never been quite top-ranked. But good; everyone said that. *Good.*

Dillon has come for items from John's collection, because his sister worries their stepmother will sell them to an archive. As Dillon speaks to Susannah about his siblings, he remembers John's relationship with their mother: his drinking, serious and steady; their quarrels; and a car wreck, revealing the affair, prompting this less cumbrous mode of life, near the beach.

For the kids, as could be expected, things were less dreamy. Dillon, along with Sonny and Helena, moved in with their maternal grandparents in Illinois, where their mother returned to school; soon after, their father won a major literary award.

Dillon recalls his mother doing gigwork when the children were little, "typing theses late at night, theses and dissertations with hundreds of footnotes." John wondered why she took on such drudgery, though he wasn't much for financial prudence himself, and relied on Dillon's mother to balance the budget (Ross Justice, "Graduate School," 124-5; Snodgrass 129). Later, Dillon's mom married again—a swaggering hothead—and became a teacher, then split from him when the kids were grown.

Dillon and Susannah walk through John's office. Susannah describes the poet's workflow system—drafts here, correspondence there—and points to a "basket on the floor," exclaiming,

[p]eople were always sending him manuscripts, including people he didn't know! I begged him not to bother with

them after his health declined, but he looked at every one of them. Just in case it was some real undiscovered talent, I guess.

According to Susannah, John worked best in the wee hours, under the sway of what he called the *"dark forces"*). Without prompting, she insists to Dillon (and to no one in particular) that John, married with children, stuck in a mid-career rut, "needed something new"—and that she had "stimulated him." She says that "[h]e did some of his best work after we got together," because she let go of her creative interests. "I made his life my work, my *art*. I understood what he was doing. The *imperishable* word, the imperishable line, that was what he was after."

But Susannah hasn't quite said her piece. Fearing that Dillon will leave, she adds, after an interval, that John "was terrible the last year or two. Simply awful," though she "forgave him" for it.

Unsure of how to right the conversation, Dillon picks up his share of his father's estate, and Helena's, too, although this upsets Susannah, who has expected her to visit. Dillon wonders if "the dark forces" was really John's phrase for his nocturnal urge to write, or if it came, instead, from Susannah. He remembers, too, reading "carefully written letters" from his father, addressed to all the children, and evincing "the value, possibly too high a value, that he put on his own experiences," since "[h]e expected the letters to be saved." Dillon has obliged him in this.

The story ends with small revelations. Dillon wonders if he'll relay Susannah's grief over John's cruelty to his mother, who "would try hard not to be glad" at the news, but who "would see it as just." He realizes he feels no lasting anger toward Susannah, though he wants to, somehow, on his mother's behalf. Or is he fond of her? The narrator adds this final report of Dillon's consciousness:

> It came to him that he'd read probably less than half his father's work. Maybe he'd catch up now. Not in the editions in the trunk, but in the everyday books on his shelves at home. Stanzas perhaps not imperishable, but good, waiting patiently all these years, hidden by so much else. He gave a small mental wince, a mental shrug. But for the moment it was all behind him, back in Susannah's keeping, and he sped along peacefully through the patchy sun and shade of the avenue.

I've summarized "The Dark Forces" in detail because it echoes—embroiders, rejiggers—so much of Donald Justice's life in poetry, his legacy and its interpersonal complexities.

Jean Ross married Donald not long after the Second World War; they had one son together, Nathaniel, who now lives in North Carolina. Like John, Donald (and Jean) made homes for a spell in South Florida, in and around Miami. Like John, Donald won a big prize—the Pulitzer, in 1979, along with the Lamont (for his first book), the Bollingen, in 1991, and the Lannan, in 1996. Like John, Don sold his papers to a library, at the University of Delaware, and kept first editions of his own and his friends' works. Like John, Don sought the *imperishable* word, but for many critics, he was merely "good" or not even that (Bedient 475).

All that said, the story's power derives from its *obversion* to reports of Donald and Jean's years together. Unlike John,

Don never remarried. Unlike John, Don was a man of putatively abstemious personal habits (Sullivan). Don's books moved to the University of Delaware, as far as I can tell, without incident.

"The Dark Forces" is a story of receptions, audiences. John/Don composes letters with one eye for the literary scholar; Dillon vows to spend more time with the work of a man he half-knew. Susannah wants *someone* to hear what her days were like with John. It's a trope that the writer depends on the reader, is the desperate one in the dyad, but Ross Justice takes that conceit and refuses the salves—that, for example, someone, somewhere will find John's work and be changed by it.

Don Justice was interested in these same questions of the posthumous; see his "The Sunset Maker," which talks about musical composition and Pierre Bonnard but is equally about the horror of being unheard (Ford). But of course Don genuinely had a public, laureled career. By contrast, Jean's life as a published writer mostly began after Don stopped, excepting a few significant short story publications. In this way Jean *is* Susannah—who, by admission, has abandoned her proper art, her self-directed writerly practice, to assume management of John's. Being some combination of a personal assistant, a counselor, a librarian, and a critic, she runs his home office and manages his afterlife.

As it happens, a great many of Jean Ross Justice's stories bear on this question of career—how one makes such a thing in the arts; how it changes over time; and what happens when an author leaves stacks of paper for others to sift through. I'm going to point to two more stories, one that reverses the gender identities of writer and subordinate, and one that replaces a corpus of texts with the soft tissue of the body.

✝ ✝ ✝

"The Next to Last Line," also from *The End of a Good Party*, dramatizes the appropriation of language. At a conference to discuss the work of a student named Sean Smith, Bettina Thayer, a visiting professor of poetry at a nameless university, is unimpressed by Sean's recent efforts. She asks after a previous piece of his, "The Beach House," and admits that "one line of that poem really stuck in my mind. . . . I liked it so much—well, in fact, I borrowed it and put it in a poem. I hope," she adds, "you're flattered."

Sean wonders how to square this with his own work— he wants to keep the line for himself—but Bettina offers to dedicate *her* poem to Sean, as compensation. Sean says he'll consider it, and the story moves ahead to a weekend party at Bettina's house. Students gossip, music plays. The party draws to a close and Sean hangs back, talking to Bettina. He admits he doesn't really want her to use his line, and she, in turn, reveals that she's *already* sent her poem out to a publication; they plan to run it. She repeats that she'll dedicate the poem to him, and he asks for a clarifying footnote instead. She offers to read her version aloud, from the sofa, but Sean is insulted that she finds her own writing superior to his— when indeed hers is buoyed by his. She apologizes and they change the subject. The conversation becomes more intimate; they have sex. The next morning, Sean accepts Bettina's dedication and leaves.

Neither Sean nor Bettina let on to the writing program about their dalliance, although it doesn't continue, and Sean acknowledges, halfway to himself, that he hoped it would. He can't decide whether or not their time together was "a simple transaction" for the line, and he worries he was insufficiently "practiced" in bed. Bettina departs at the end of the semester, and a new visiting lecturer ("a man of moderate reputation") arrives. The story jumps ahead to Sean's final conference with him:

> [H]e said to Sean, "Teaching's a funny business. You can be so wrong. I've seen people I thought had very modest talents make it pretty big. It's partly just sticking with it, working like a dog. Maybe you don't know whose talent *is* modest till later on." It sounded wise; but had the guy been trying to send him a message?
>
> A copy of Bettina Thayer's last book came, not from her with an inscription, but from the publisher, with a card that said "Compliments of the author." He found the poem dedicated to himself; his name on the page gave him a little *frisson* of feeling. A pretty good poem, his line neatly fitted in. If it was any longer his line.
>
> When anyone asked later why he'd left the program and enrolled in law school, he would say, "Oh, it was all so competitive. Maybe I'll keep it up on my own."

At home with his wife years later, Sean mentions the incident; his wife finds Bettina's actions fascinating and manipulative. Sean drifts off to sleep, contemplating a poem, toying with phrases: *"that line of mine you lusted for one night. . . ."*

"The Offer" presents another form of giving, with drastically higher stakes. A husband, a wife, and their mutual friend, all unnamed, live near each other in an Iowa City-like town. The husband and friend are departmental colleagues. Their friend is gravely sick with renal disease, and after a dinner at the couple's home, the wife—substantially younger than both men—tells her husband she'd like to give the man one of her kidneys. The husband mulls this over for days, and experiences a range of emotions—anger, confusion, concern. "Her new idea," he thinks to himself, is "beyond generosity and beyond most friendships." He recalls his colleague's demeanor, when he was acting department chair: slow to anger, and patient among the squabblers comprising the university's liberal arts faculty. He also remembers his anxiety at bringing his wife to campus events—he fears she's intellectually undistinguished, though he has given her things to read to broaden her horizons. But the wife, like the friend, maintains a sunny disposition around her increasingly gloomy husband.

Gradually, the husband entertains his jealousies: he worries his wife and the friend are having an affair (the man was, in health, a "skirt-chaser"). He can't conceive of how the town and school would respond to news that his wife, and not his colleague, has given a kidney to an all-too-deserving, mild-mannered person. He keeps asking if his wife will *actually* do it; she keeps saying she will. She reminds him to call the friend, to see how he's doing, but he can't. He's consumed by the pair's arrangement, its disarming intimacies.

The friend dies. His wife reveals, on preparing to attend the man's memorial, that she *did* in fact offer the kidney, but the friend declined. The husband sits in church, wrestling with his, and his wife's, capacities for care:

> It was necessary to have trust. What was marriage without trust? He closed his eyes, as determinedly as if he would never open them again. Nothing had happened. What if it had? What if people knew? (And smiled because he

didn't?) No one knew, and anyway, his friend was dead, very dead. Which he would certainly never consider a relief. Never.

I'll confess that Bettina's stratagem feels to me like empowerment, or like power plain and simple. Sean can't remember if the words were really so lambent after all, worth the trouble they've caused him, days and nights spent fretting. For Bettina, language comes easily, from her own mind and, occasionally, from a student's, but even the most scrupulous poets know that that's to be expected. (Don, in this sense, was overscrupulous. His attentiveness to sourcing, his feelings of belatedness, are famous. [Martin passim]) Sean vows to write a latter-day poem of revenge—it feels hopeless, a little pathetic, as though Bettina will care (or read it). Bettina may be a "24-7 relentless careerist" (Behrle), but careerism here has a neutral sense, and lord knows that men have stolen their share of good lines from partners and classmates. The story toggles between critique and admiration—perhaps *the* emotional dialectic of any writing workshop.

"The Offer" slips from poets to humanities professors, and the patriarchal norms are mostly reestablished. The young wife wants to give of herself to a man who isn't her husband; she provides not the comfort of an amanuensis but that of a donor, a literal lifeline. Here, marriage is defined not only by what one gives to one's spouse, but by what one doesn't give to anyone else. To be married to a university man is to be wanting—not steeped enough in the state of the academic field—and to be overzealous, too eager to step over the boundaries that carve up the college. Keep your organs in your own body, the husband says. (It's fascinating to note, too, that the husband's first wife was a "plumber with a liberal arts degree," a lover of ideas with no professional stake in them.) "The Offer" problematizes control, the core of the abusive, or here at minimum asymmetric, relational dynamic. Even the most assiduous of controlling partners finds he cannot account for everything in his partner's mind. Her wishes eventually elude him. He can't keep her body intact—he can't hold the corpus together.

Reputations, we're told, are a tricky business; poetic afterlives are cruel. The lion's share of Justice's papers aren't even categorized at the University of Delaware library, though I've tried at times to nudge them along. Money, first, and human-power second are required to care about and for a writer after they've passed. Indeed, it takes a fair amount of both to care about one's own work while one's living, which is why Sean's proto-career peters out—he can't be bothered, ultimately, to defend the products of his mind. And maybe they weren't totally his; in a conversation between writers, it's hard to ascertain what belongs to whom.

"The Offer" is my favorite of Jean's stories—I love its bitterness, the gentle (free) indirection of its ending, where the husband glories over the death of another man and pushes aside concerns about his wife's behavior. People can say what they want, he thinks; the best art is being alive, or living longer.

These stories, I've long felt, metabolize the patriarchal poison. They're also a space for creative concerns, and it's reductive to imagine them as a point-for-point critique of husbands in general or even Ross Justice's beloved husband, whose work means so much to me and to many. They're occasions, after all, for subtlety, not polemic. And yet. The men here always come out looking silly—they *are* silly. Their poems are forgotten, and their children haven't even really read them.

As I went through Don Justice's letters in the reading room of the Morris Library, I marveled at their voice, their testament to a good nature—*and* their litany of complaints. The food at Yaddo, this or that correction to a galley, the outcome of a hand of poker. His colds, his clothes, money. Sometimes, without any right to be, I was annoyed on Jean's behalf. She was doing the work of buoying the man *before*, or at least alongside, the work of inventing herself as an artist.

No one gets into, or back into, a period of sustained creativity just to settle scores, even small ones. It's too painful to write, too lonely and alienating. But if one finds oneself with a little more time, without the responsibilities of looking after a partner and child; and if in that little, dear time one begins again to compose things beautiful and true, to gain well-deserved notoriety for them, however belated, and is celebrated for one's proper achievement after years of being thanked in the backs of books for the stewardship of someone else's ideas and runny noses and page-proofs. . . .

And if, in the course of drafting those stories, some counter- or para-factual writing creeps in, writing on a different plane, in which characters criticize their late partners or get the glorious lines for themselves (because those lines might indeed have been theirs at the start), or give what they alone can give to a person who's not their husband. . . .

If, to say it plainly, those stories right some wrongs and reverse some asymmetries. . . .

Isn't that understandable—and isn't that radical art?

....

CHRISTIAN SCHLEGEL is the author of two books of poetry: *Honest James* (The Song Cave, 2015) and *ryman* (Ricochet, forthcoming 2022). He holds an MFA from the Iowa Writers' Workshop and a PhD from Harvard, and teaches English at Pierrepont School in Westport, CT. He lives in New Haven.

WORKS CITED

Calvin Bedient, "New Confessions," *The Sewanee Review*, 88.3, Summer 1980, 474-88.

Jim Behrle, "24-7 Relentless Careerism," *The Poetry Foundation* online, March 8, 2010, https://www.poetryfoundation.org/articles/69501/24-7-relentless-careerism, n.p.

Mark Ford, "Erasures," *The London Review of Books*, 28.22, November 16, 2006, https://www.lrb.co.uk/the-paper/v28/n22/mark-ford/erasures, n.p.

Dana Gioia and William Logan, eds. *Certain Solitudes: On the Poetry of Donald Justice* (Fayetteville: Arkansas UP, 1997).

Jean Ross Justice, "The Dark Forces," *The Yale Review*, 93.1, January 2005, 144-56.

_____, *The End of a Good Party and Other Stories* (Tampa: Tampa UP, 2008).

_____, "Graduate School: The Thin Young Man," *Certain Solitudes*, 117-26.

Walter Martin, "Arts of Departure," *Certain Solitudes*, 37-52.

W. D. Snodgrass, "Justice as Classmate," *Certain Solitudes*, 129-32.

John Jeremiah Sullivan, "Donald Justice's 'There Is a Gold Light in Certain Old Paintings,'" *The Paris Review* online, Dec. 1, 2011, https://www.theparisreview.org/blog/2011/12/01/there-is-a-gold-light-in-certain-old-paintings/, n.p.

DISPLACING THE HOUSEWIFE IN *ESQUIRE*: JEAN ROSS JUSTICE'S "AN OLD MAN'S WINTER NIGHT"

Michael Smolinsky

In the late 1950s, Jean Ross Justice's stories were published alongside those of some of the biggest prose writers in America—and in one of the most widely distributed mass-market magazines in the country: *Esquire: The Magazine for Men.* At the time, *Esquire* positioned itself not only as a magazine for men, but for men who liked serious writing. Two of Justice's stories were published in 1959 alongside work by writers including Kingsley Amis and Norman Mailer. Soon after this auspicious start, however, Justice's work stopped appearing in the magazine.

Possibly the demands of motherhood got in the way, as her son Nathaniel was born shortly thereafter. Perhaps the career of her husband, the late poet Donald Justice, took precedence in their household; he had earned his doctorate from the University of Iowa in 1954 and was teaching there by the late 1950s. But beyond these personal circumstances, how might the nature of the publishing industry and the literary tastes it cultivated at the time have impacted her career?

Justice's stories fit—albeit uncomfortably—within the magazine's editorial strategy as described in Kenon Breazeale's oft-cited 1994 article, "In Spite of Women: *Esquire* Magazine and the Construction of the Male Consumer," especially the way *Esquire* constructed masculinity and femininity through the 1930s, '40s, and '50s. Justice seems to have taken as the starting point for her story the kind of reader *Esquire* was trying to cultivate: middle-class, financially comfortable, looking to fill new-found leisure time, and in charge of purchasing items for the domestic space—liberated from the control of a bossy wife.

While "In Spite of Women" is more focused on *Esquire's* visual images, Brazeale's holistic approach is a useful one for interpreting the magazine's written content as well: "Magazines are calculated packages of meaning whose aim is to transform the reader into an imaginary subject—as Louis Althusser put it, to 'appellate' each reader. Magazines are both devised and experienced as a whole and meaningfully studied as a system entire" (p. 9). By paying similar attention to the historical context and material object in which Justice's *Esquire* stories were published, we might appreciate the ways her writing reinforces, resists, and/or redirects the magazine's strategy, deepening our understanding of her work and the trajectory of her career.

The main challenge faced by *Esquire*, according to Brazeale, was that "Most of the activities being touted [in its pages]—cooking, interior decoration, and so on—were by definition fatally associated with housewifery" (p. 6). Those associations had been established by enormously popular and profitable magazines such as *Ladies Home Journal, Vogue,* and *Harper's Bazaar* in the decades before *Esquire* was launched in 1933—during the Great Depression, ironically. In order for *Esquire* to open up a space for the consuming male, it had to "displace that archetype of consuming femininity, the housewife" (p. 10). (See figure 1).

Figure 1. Advertisement in March 1959 issue of *Esquire*

Justice's "An Old Man's Winter Night," which appeared in the March 1959 issue of *Esquire*, is a story of just such a displacement—though one experienced not as liberation but as a haunting. She deftly incorporates elements of the Southern Gothic mode, including its tension between natural and supernatural elements, and its dark humor, into this story about the hollowing out of the "woman-identified associations so firmly lodged at the center of America's commodified domestic environment."

Justice's familiarity with and interest in Southern Gothic literature was deep; in fact, had she finished her graduate degree at University of North Carolina, Justice would have written one of the first theses on William Faulkner, arguably the most important practitioner of the genre. One of the hallmarks of Southern Gothic is the "Freudian return of the repressed" in which "the region's historical realities take concrete forms in the shape of ghosts that highlight all that has been unsaid in the official version of southern history" with its pastoralism ("Southern Gothic Literature," *Oxford Research Encyclopedia*). While "An Old Man's Winter Night" is certainly lighter in tone and subject matter than most work by Southern Gothic writers such as Faulkner or Carson McCullers, we might see Justice's story as similarly marked by a return of the repressed, in which the idyllic vision of bourgeois American domesticity, prosperity, and masculinity imagined by *Esquire* is haunted by the displaced housewife (and the specter of scarcity).

In the first sentence of Justice's story, we learn that "Mr. George Crayton, a widower who lived alone, was awakened one cold November night by a sound somewhere in his house." That sentence is also the entire first paragraph: the fact that George is a widower who lives alone is the most important aspect of his character.

In a sense George is a typical *Esquire* man, but Justice has found an aporia in the demographic: bachelors are not the only single male consumers; so are widowers. What the reader goes on to encounter in "An Old Man's Winter Night" is no bachelor pad filled with urbane conversation, well-tailored suits, masculine cocktails, and sexually liberated women, as in the pages of the magazine, but a place "*silent as the grave.*" Because *Esquire* was targeting the single man at the younger end of life—the bachelor—telling a story about a single man at the other end of life is a way of turning a mirror upon *Esquire* itself. Justice's story is funny and insightful by its very structure—that is, through its ingenious substitution of widower for bachelor—and must have gained additional depth when read by an audience of (mostly) bachelors.

"An Old Man's Winter's Night" literalizes the magazine's editorial strategy and then troubles it, slyly commenting on and turning it to Justice's own ends as a woman and a professional writer. Ultimately, she succeeded in that she published a formidable piece of short fiction in a magazine with a circulation of approximately 800,000 and an advertising base (and presumably, an editorial budget) that would have dwarfed any literary journal of its day.

I suspect that one of the reasons she did not continue to be published in the magazine's pages was that she was both a serious writer *and* a woman. In contrast, Dorothy Parker's long-standing book review column for *Esquire* was sophisticated but superficial—however self-conscious and performative that frivolity may have been. In the same issue in which "An Old Man's Winter's Night" appeared, Parker plays the dithering woman: "Now just today at lunch time . . . I could not decide whether to order lemon sole or mushroom omelet. There seemed to be so much to say on both sides.

As a result, while I was conscientiously listing the opposing claims, the restaurant closed for the afternoon, and I am still hungry. . . . And today, again, I am in bad trouble about the two books that are burning holes in my table."

After George Crayton is awakened in the middle of the night, he feels "the cold air of the room on his uncovered ears." You have to slow down to notice the odd detail of "on his uncovered ears" and appreciate how effectively it brings you right next to George's skin and conveys that George's entire consciousness is in his ears during that tense moment.

George leaves his bedroom, enters the dining room—the place for entertaining guests—yells, "Halt!" and finds that someone has cut the lights: "The room was icy, and the stillness was as deep as the darkness—*silent as the grave* was what flashed across his mind. Perhaps the room was empty after all, and he had only been hearing things again." And yet, in the story's striking and central twist, George finds himself in that moment desiring company: "As he strained his eyes into the dark, he hoped desperately that there was someone there. The failure of the lights had begun to seem more than peculiar; it was unnatural, even a little ghostly. He thought of how he had been saying to people, ever since his wife died, 'I'm ready to go, whenever my time comes!' What a damned lie!"

When George finally turns on the light in the bedroom, he sees a tall, well-built man . . . wearing a cloth mask, the chalky color of a clown's face, but it was meant to be scary." The man raises his hands in the air "slowly and somewhat lazily—but without prompting, as if it were a matter of etiquette." The suggestion that putting up one's hands is a matter of etiquette seems to satirize the prescriptive masculinity within the magazine's pages, as if the *Esquire Etiquette Book* advertised in the issue advised readers that "When burgling someone's home, take care not to frighten women or children, and if discovered by the man of the house, by all means 'Put your hands up,' as they say in the gangster films; even if Mr. Smith intends you no grievous harm, a gesture of surrender is a sign of respect."

George briefly admonishes the burglar ("You're one of Jim Tomlinson's boys . . . He'd skin you alive if he knew what you was up to"), asks him to put on a pot of coffee, and returns to the bedroom to change out of his pajamas, as you would on such an occasion: "He was about to step into his everyday brogans, but opened the closet door and pulled out a pair of felt bedroom slippers—a present from his wife that he had little occasion to use." The sartorial deliberation here heightens the satire nicely, with the bedroom slippers as the capper. In addition to advertisements and articles on liquor, footwear features prominently throughout the issue; bedroom slippers are exactly the kind of luxury item that *Esquire* wanted its readers to buy for themselves. In this case, though, it was George's late wife who purchased them.

George, in contrast, remains tight-fisted, noting at the start that "They thought he had money. Sometimes it made him laugh when he thought how sure everybody was that he had money, how some people even twitted him about being so stingy with it! Of course he had a little put by; anybody might, after working hard all a lifetime. But they must think he had pots of it buried somewhere on the place." It is as if his late wife were buried with their savings and so remains the posthumous holder of the family purse-strings. Later in the story, George says to the burglar "Guess I'll have to get me a watchdog . . . To keep off the stragglers. And the salesmen. Half the people I see is these blamed salesmen."

After chatting with the burglar, George puts more wood on the fire and notices a particularly long, heavy piece of hickory, which he places off to the side in case an opportunity to hit the intruder/guest should present itself. But George is more absorbed by what he would tell the neighbors: "He did not picture to himself the actual striking of the blow, but he thought of how his arrival at the neighbors' would be: he would rouse the Wadleys and call out matter-of-factly, 'Hate to bother you folks like this, but I got a fellow tied up over at my place—broke in my house this morning." Here, I think, one can imagine how the magazine's strategy of cultivating a self-conscious masculinity might have opened a door to seeing masculinity as constructed or performed—might have provided Justice with an opportunity to explore, with humor and sympathy, the ways that men are also constrained by gender roles and perform their maleness through, for example, showing the world that they are willing to violently defend their property.

Furthermore, we might see the substitution of "intruder" for "guest" as another inversion (similar to the substitution of widower for bachelor) through which Justice turns a mirror on *Esquire* and its ideal reader: while the magazine sells an ideal of entertaining for welcome guests, George hosts an unwelcome one—an intruder.

She develops this theme of conflicted masculine domesticity more fully towards the end of the story, in what might be considered the comic climax. When the coffee is finally ready, George pulls two cups from the pantry and wonders "for the first time about what he was doing. Was he going to give the man coffee and then try to hit him over the head? Giving him coffee couldn't be justified on the grounds of putting him off guard—it would be likely to make him more alert, if anything. Well, let it go hang! He knew he wouldn't do anything with that stick of hickory wood, except maybe put it on the stove. Let them all go hang—the Wadleys and the old men in town . . . he would never be able to tell the story to a living soul—but to hell with that. He meant to enjoy his coffee." I would suggest that George is very much an *Esquire* man—he is a gentleman, a good host, well-mannered, and he values refinement and pleasure, not just physical prowess—even if the editors might have been uncomfortable acknowledging it.

The humor is followed by a moment of real tenderness, at least on George's part: "'Sugar bowl around here somewhere, but blessed if I know where. No woman in the house, and I don't *entertain* much.' He poured the coffee. 'I buried a mighty good woman about seven years ago.'" In response, the burglar yawns and actually falls asleep! George rouses him lightly and offers him some more coffee. When the man leaves, he says, "I be seeing you, Mr. George." George's response is clearly for the benefit of the neighbors: "'Better not be, not at nighttime here on this place, you hear that?' Mr. George said after the screen door had slammed."

Esquire had taken the editorial formula of popular women's magazines while simultaneously satirizing women's taste: "Not surprisingly, some in the journalism fraternity began identifying the feminine with gullible vulnerability to consumerism's trashy faddishness. Throughout the 1920s a humorous discourse evolved that equated women's winning the vote with their gaining unbridled power as consumers. Male pundits (the best known being H. L. Mencken and Harold Nicholson) expressed a wide-ranging hostility toward women's (inferior) tastes and tendencies coming to dominate the cultural marketplace" (p. 4). Justice's writing was not

207

going to function well as "a foil against which a superior male taste could be posited" (p. 8). More than that, Justice was willing and able to satirize the emerging conventions and contradictions of American men's magazines, especially their vision of a bourgeois American man defined on the one hand by the newfangled activities of shopping and entertaining and on the other by the traditional ability and willingness to defend the home; who on the one hand was liberated from or no longer needed women, but at the same time desired women.

That she was able to publish, as a woman writer in the 1950s, a story of this depth and subtlety in a mass-market men's magazine—and a story that so entertainingly plays with and satirizes the very conventions of that magazine—confirms for me that Jean Ross Justice was a master. I hope that she was paid handsomely, and that her work will be more widely circulated and read closely in the future.

....

MICHAEL SMOLINSKY is a medical writer with a PhD in English from the University of Iowa and an MFA in poetry from Rutgers-Newark.

JEAN ROSS JUSTICE'S "THE SKY FADING UPWARD TO YELLOW: A FOOTNOTE TO LITERARY HISTORY"

Lan Samantha Chang

Jean Ross Justice's superb "The Sky Fading Upward to Yellow: A Footnote to Literary History" was recommended to me by a friend, the poet Nan Cohen. She had discovered the story ten years earlier, in the *O. Henry Prize Anthology* in 1989, and had revisited it many times before sharing it with me. "The Sky Fading Upward to Yellow" has a way of haunting its readers. In the two decades since I encountered it, this story has held a singular place in my mind as an assiduously observed, precisely rendered sliver of a fading world in which I was a graduate student in the early 1990s: a world that has, at this point, largely vanished.

The story is told in the aftermath of the death of the distinguished novelist Robert Worsham. In the course of its pages, his former graduate students, Rachel and Brenda, wrestle with the question of whether Brenda should reveal to Worsham's biographer, Dozier, the details of the affair she had with Worsham during their year as student and teacher. This question leads Rachel to explore why she believes the story should not be revealed.

I've always imagined that "The Sky Fading Upward to Yellow" was set in Iowa City, where I went to school. The river in the story is the Iowa River. The museum is the old University of Iowa Museum of Art. The footbridge, where Worsham and Brenda paused to view the colors of the winter sky, and where he gave her a toy ring, still spans the river between the old museum and the side of the river where the Iowa Writers' Workshop is located. But in truth, the story has its own life independent from that program. Although Jean Ross Justice made her home there for decades with her husband, Donald Justice, who was the cornerstone of the Workshop's poetry program until the early 1980s, the couple lived in several college towns over the course of their fifty-seven-year marriage. "The Sky Fading Upward to Yellow" could have taken place in any academic setting, because its depiction of the student writers—who long to see, to know, to *become* the distinguished writer—is universal.

The story's prose is remarkable for its needle-like, discerning observations of these young writers. They're eager to know Worsham's literary opinions, to discover whose work he thinks is "Good;" but they're also scanning for his personal history, his strengths and vulnerabilities. The student dinner guests eye the famous writer more hungrily than the plates of food they balance on their laps. They note his body shape, his walk, his views on women's fashions. They sense immediately that there is something going on between Brenda and Worsham, because he "seemed to know where everything was in [her] kitchen without having to ask."

Rachel, the narrator, relates some years later the protectiveness she and her classmates developed toward their married teacher and his infidelity. "And soon we all felt too loyal to pass judgment. In some odd way, the affair with Brenda might have seemed to make him more one of us." When Worsham returns to his wife Madeleine, the affair becomes an invisible plot point in the official narrative of his personal life. While they loyally keep his secret, the students struggle on their own, years after his death, to figure out what it all meant.

Rachel is an editor at a wildlife magazine. Her literary dreams, like those of most in her graduate class, have not been fulfilled. She refers to the university town as a place of unrealized ambitions, "where we'd gone expecting, like so many others, to become writers." Much of "The Sky Fading Upward to Yellow" inhabits a series of conversations in the aftermath of Worsham's death.

In the story's first scene, Rachel is visiting Brenda, who has stayed in the town where she and Worsham were once together. Rachel and Brenda's friend Jed sit in Whaley's, the tavern they frequented in graduate school, and listen as Brenda, her legs stretched across the opposite booth, recalls moments from her relationship with Worsham and anticipates a call from Dozier. Both Jed and Rachel assure Brenda that, of course, she will be contacted. Jed, whom Rachel speculates admires Brenda as "'a remarkable woman, gifted and vital, once mistress of a famous novelist,'" asserts to Rachel that any biographer of Worsham must interview Brenda because "She's the one who was closest to him that year. She knows things nobody else would know. What he was thinking about. His inner life."

But Brenda does not hear from Dozier. A few years later, reading excerpts from his biography of Worsham, Rachel comes across a short passage about the year Worsham taught her and her classmates. Though brief and unrevealing, the excerpt brings Rachel to a moment of nostalgic recollection of "how fine that year had been, even finer than we'd known at the time. It made me happy and sad." Brenda, reading the same passage, responds, "So much missing!" She resolves to write her own account, justifying herself by pointing out that a description of their affair would give the world access to important information about the composition of Worsham's final novel, as well as the book that remained unfinished when he died.

As the story unfolds, Rachel and Brenda consider the question over visits, memories, and phone calls: Should Brenda offer her journal and letters to Dozier? Should she reveal the affair, even though it might be "a breach of taste or judgement," uncomfortable or painful to Worsham's widow, Madeleine, who might not know of Brenda's existence? Should Brenda tell her story, for the sake of literary history? After all, as Brenda points out, her year with Worsham was "a pretty important time," one of the last productive years of the novelist's life.

But Brenda's desires make Rachel uneasy, and she tries to forestall Brenda's resolution: "Maybe you should let it sit for a while and see how it looks later." This silence, this refusal to encourage her friend, is one of Rachel's more active moments in the story; the other is her response, sometime later, when Brenda reads her written account of the affair with Worsham aloud—when Rachel first knows that she is "sick of [Brenda's] important recollections." As Brenda continues to describe the affair, Rachel silently recalls her own private observations of Worsham during that year: his "tight, secretive walk," when he is unaware that anyone is observing him, hands in his pockets, "pondering lives known to him only, fictional people and events he was trying to understand and shape. That glimpse of him always gave me a moment of deep happiness."

In her quieter, even stealthier way, Rachel treasures Worsham as much as Brenda does. When she tries to discourage Brenda, Brenda insinuates that Rachel is jealous, asserting that if Rachel had had the experience, she would spill the information. Rachel declares she never would; this vow gives her "a mysterious thrill." She encourages Brenda to turn the piece into fiction, placating her, telling her "you might make something really good out of it." When the story ends, Dozier's biography has been published without Brenda's account. Rachel buys the biography at noon, brings it home, and reads it before she eats her lunch, but finds it "empty of the old excitement." After speaking to Brenda, she considers Brenda's desire to offer her letters and memoir to Dozier "ridiculous" and "unseemly." Instead, she resolves to rely on Worsham's novels: "Here he is. This is all we need."

When I first read "The Sky Fading Upwards to Yellow," I was still a youngish writer, naïve and curious about the lives of artists, drawn into this fascinating and precisely written account of a woman's role in the life of literary genius in an era when literary genius was mostly male. I was especially aware of the extent to which Rachel and her classmates take the primacy of the male genius for granted. In the world of this story, the women surrounding male genius are given importance only as curators of the male writer's personal story and literary reputation. As Rachel notes in the story's opening, the death of a distinguished novelist is thus the kind of a situation in which his wife finally holds the power, gets her "day in court." The wife, or "long-term alliance," control the literary legacy and life story of that male genius. It is the widow, Madeleine's, "due" that she be given the right to curate his letters, to carefully eliminate any references to the marital discord that Brenda experienced firsthand. And Brenda's desire to claim her right as a "short-term alliance," to have a page in Worsham's biography, puts Madeleine's power at risk.

Rachel chooses to see the issue as personal: as a disappointment in which Brenda wants or expects more from Worsham than she has the right to receive. But when she suggests to Brenda that things might have been so different if she had "found" Worsham in his own youth, as a fellow student sitting next to her in class, Brenda reacts to this more defensively than she has at any point in the story: "Oh, you think I was drawn to his success? I can tell you, name and fame were not in it. I'd have seen him for what he was anywhere. Reflected glory is *not* my thing." Her suspicions reveal a subtext that perhaps she did, indeed, long for reflected glory. What *was* her thing? Rachel assumes, again, that this is personal, that Brenda's desire to share her letters and information from her affair with Worsham springs from a long-ago disappointment. "Oh, doesn't every woman, no matter how often she's said they're free, doesn't she, deep down, expect the man freely to give up all the others for her?. . . . But she wanted more: a page in his history, a paragraph, a footnote. She may have felt it was a kind of belated gift that he'd have wanted her to have."

Rachel recounts a road trip to New York, where Worsham lived, that she and Brenda took during spring vacation in the year of the affair. When Rachel wonders whether Worsham is also in New York, Brenda passionately declares to Rachel that she believes in the "freedom" of their relationship, implying that what they have together is significant beyond the conventions of marriage. For her own part, Rachel assumes that any woman who would pursue a married man must understand that she would dwell in glimpses, in ephemerality, rather than in the inscribed permanence of record.

Such glimpses make a powerful impression, not only on Brenda, whom Rachel describes as someone who "dealt more in moments than continuity," but on Rachel herself. She recalls Brenda's description of walking with Worsham across a footbridge after a visit to a museum. The changing winter light, "the sky fading upward to yellow." "The sky fading upward to yellow!" Rachel repeats, admitting, "I'd been caught up in the account in spite of myself. . . ." The phrase itself unlocks her own private glimpse of Worsham in a moment when he thinks no one is watching.

She considers the sublimity of the affair. "I thought of them sitting side by side in a booth in Whaley's, smiling with an unanimity of gaze and an air of great happiness, as if they'd just had some wonderful news." As a somewhat self-conscious and awkward-feeling Midwesterner, a woman Worsham himself deemed "too level-headed and sensible" to have been in Brenda's situation, Rachel wonders at Brenda's desire to make the relationship public. "Wasn't it enough? It wasn't, thank God, my job to sort out what this meant in their lives in the long run, but there it was, it had happened, with all its joy of discovery."

When Rachel is talking Brenda out of making her memoir public, she suggests that the transformation into fiction might make it "good." In the context of their faded literary dreams, this is a poignant echo of their graduate school fascination with what is "Good." Perhaps Rachel is also gently, or not so gently, suggesting that Brenda may have lost sight of what is "good." Coming right before the white space, as it does, the remark shows sincerity about aiming high, but also an edge, implying that what Rachel has written is not good yet. It is also keen in its depiction of the complexity of the characters and their relationship, a friendship rooted in the pursuit of the "good" but also a very human friendship.

As a young writer reading the story fifteen years after it was written and many more after the story was set, I believed I understood the subtext of Brenda's desire: an aspiration for literary success, a wistful yearning to be seen. Brenda is described in Rachel's student journals as "an aloof exhibitionist . . . she wanted our attention, then seemed to throw it away." Rereading the story as an older writer, I am reminded that in any time, the vast majority of writers are not read. They build their lives around inner worlds that are not widely shared; like Brenda, they do not make a public literary contribution.

Brenda wanted—perhaps still wants—to be a writer. It is not mentioned that Brenda has ever published a single story or poem, yet she has gone on living for years in the town where her hopes flamed brightest, and her affair with Robert Worsham remains, in many ways, the highlight of her artistic life. Years later, her artistic ambitions unfulfilled, Brenda still longs to be seen. She wants her story to finally be told, acknowledged. "The Sky Fading Upward to Yellow" is, in many ways, Rachel's argument that it should *not* be acknowledged.

Years after I first read this story subtitled "A Footnote to Literary History," I now see that Rachel's attempts to keep Brenda from revealing her story might be interpreted by many writers today as a kind of silencing that supports male literary hegemony. At the time I'm writing this, it's no longer believed that men in powerful positions deserve to have their old flings "cloaked in a decent obscurity," as Rachel's companion, Tim, suggests. Of course, Tim isn't alone in his opinion; the other students feel protective of Worsham. Andrea and Herb, the most successful writers of the class, apparently do not mention the affair to Dozier. It's possible, then, to read Rachel, Andrea, and Herb as complicit; it's possible to see that by developing a relationship with Brenda, Worsham took advantage of his power over a hopeful student who, as Tim says, want[s] to "consummate the union with Success! As if the magic will rub off on you." In this reading, "The Sky Fading Upward to Yellow" is about the erasure of Brenda's voice. This reading is persuasive; the story could effortlessly be interpreted as fortifying the power dynamics that silence women's stories. But Justice was writing in a different era with different preoccupations.

The ongoing conversation between Brenda and Rachel reveals a fascination with the privacy of the artistic life, as well as a preoccupation with the question of biography and what will survive writers after they are gone. It was written by a woman steeped for decades in an elite literary world, a woman finding her published voice at an age when most writers can no longer pretend to be youthful anymore, and in an era when many writers look to what will outlive them. Brenda and Rachel are only a few years out of graduate school at the time of their conversations, but Rachel narrates the story from a point in time long after the affair.

Justice could write with the dry-eyed clarity of the married strategist, describing a year-long romantic affair as a "short-term alliance" in comparison to the decades-long confederation of a marriage; yet, she could also write from the perspective of the curious, hopeful students in describing the evanescent magnitude of the year-long love affair. Some of the most revelatory passages of the story are about Worsham and Brenda, seen as the young Rachel had seen them. The story's greatness comes from Justice's clarity as well as her ability to penetrate the ephemeral beauty in these moments.

Rachel's stake in the privacy of Worsham's story is entirely different from Brenda's need to reveal her knowledge of his "inner life." Although Rachel struggles between valuing the undefinable, poetic relationship and the concrete, socially defined, time-tested, institutionally sanctioned marriage, she is not protecting the idea of fidelity or the widow Madeleine's feelings, but something different. She believes that telling the story would be "*unseemly.*" That Worsham's work should be read and appreciated on its own. That the weathered, middle-aged man she and her classmates knew is more real than his photograph, "handsome in his twenties"; that the private and unphotographed, middle-aged visage is "his true appearance, the way he was meant to be." To Rachel, the most significant things are private and must be kept unseen.

Rachel and Worsham once shared a coded conversation about his impending return to his wife, after his affair with Brenda. Rachel doesn't tell Brenda about it, "but hoarded it as though it were important." After Rachel recounts the deeply happy memory of Worsham walking through town, lost in his imagination, she admits, "I didn't like to think that people who hadn't read much of him or fully taken in what they read (hadn't loved it enough?) would one day be poking into the secret recesses of his life."

How fine that year had been. What was important about the affair was that it truly did exist to Rachel, Brenda, and their classmates; to them, it was the human touch of greatness. However "unseemly" it might be for Brenda to tell about the affair, Rachel still believes the experience was significant and beautiful and rare. The story is a meditation on expressing the ineffable—which is what writers do. Writers breathe within the part of life that exists in between the public pieces. Rachel believes in preserving the inexpressible, the untold. The artistic life, the secret life, belongs outside of the official story, the public life. The place for this secret life lies in art. So, as she suggested to Brenda, Rachel documents the ineffable in fiction, her own fiction. The existence of Rachel's story embodies some of the proof Brenda is hoping for; Rachel is loyal to Brenda because, presumably years later, she has remembered the story and recreated what is most important to her: its poetic significance, which will vanish when those who knew of it are gone. The toy ring. The windless, cold December afternoon. The walk over the footbridge near the museum. The sky fading upward to yellow.

....

LAN SAMANTHA CHANG is the author of *The Family Chao* and three other books of fiction. She lives with her husband and daughter in Iowa City, where she directs the Iowa Writers' Workshop.

THIS EDITION OF THE UNSUNG MASTERS
IS PRODUCED AS A COLLABORATION AMONG:

Gulf Coast: A Journal of Literature and Fine Arts
and
Copper Nickel
Pleiades: Literature in Context
The Georgia Review

GENEROUS SUPPORT AND FUNDING PROVIDED BY:

The Nancy Luton Fund
University of Houston Department of English

This book is set in Marion with Avenir
and Manifesto titles and Poiret One page numbers.